the hope grid.

susan b. roara

Publisher's note: This is a work of fiction. Names, characters, places, and incidents either are the product of the author's imagination or are used fictitiously. Any resemblance to actual events, locales, or persons, living or dead, is entirely coincidental.

Editing and ebook formatting by Kristen Corrects, Inc.
Cover art design by Nicole Bastiaanse-Fritch

First edition published 2018

ISBN: 978-0-9967822-8-9

Author's Note

Dear Reader,

It all started five years ago, long after the death of my mother. I suppose that I had always been creative, but I liked numbers more than anything.

Years after my mother passed, I sat down with my computer and opened the blank document. I felt like I was forgetting her, that her memories were becoming blurry and lost. I started writing my thoughts, mostly to preserve the emotions that I valued—the stories, the life events, the love I had for her—as best as I could because I wasn't a writer, so I thought.

That year changed me. I had written two novels and my life suddenly became fulfilled in some way.

I was never alone when I wrote. A presence could always be felt, my mother's energy unmistakable. My whole life I trusted my instincts and had mildly acknowledged that my intuition was strong. I believed in spirits, energy, and "the signs" and felt overwhelmed by

3

the level of peace and understanding that I received from them.

Writing healed me in a way that was unexpected. I realized quickly that I could transport thoughts and ideas to paper and boggle them down with other words and stories, to hide the truths of my feelings. *It was safe*, in my books, with my words. Only I held the key to their true meanings. The writing came easy. Little bumps in the road as far as technicality, but the ideas came to me, and the stories flowed.

I call myself an intuitive writer, because that's what I am. I write stories with unseen intention, but the purposes revealed are so significant to my life that it is without a doubt a gift to me.

I began writing this book, knowing I had no idea how to do so. I knew the words would come through me—they always do—but I couldn't imagine what the story would be. It was a complicated subject, one I hoped to simplify respectfully and with integrity.

My brother's death, the whole thing was a tragic mistake. He never meant to die. But kids do stupid things and make mistakes; it's a part of life.

I'll never forget the morning I saw Thomas' face in the mirror. I took a great pause and stared at myself and said, "God! I look just like Tom." I realized days later, after the initial shock of his death had started to wear, that it was *him* in the mirror. That his image came to me, and that was the last image I had of him, staring back at me.

I wrote this story, knowing that the message and gifts from this book were significant.

My goal was to give purpose and meaning to the life of a peculiar boy whose humor I hoped to capture, whose wit and smile resembled mine in many ways. He was here to help me; his hand graced mine as we wrote, and together we pass along the lessons of his life in hopes that it will help and heal others.

Susan B. Roara

Books by Susan B. Roara

The Right Family
My Mother's Gift
Vintage Hearts

the hope grid.

susan b. roara

For my soul family, for those I have met and for those I have yet to discover.

My deepest love.

My deepest gratitude.

DRAGONFLY

*The dragonfly is the keeper of dreams that reminds us that
anything is possible. Dragonflies inspire spirituality and creativity;
they help us on the path of discovery and enlightenment. The
dragonfly navigates with elegance and grace.*

Native American saying

Chapter
One

SB+JY.

Bold letters were etched on the wall halfway up to the ceiling, fading in permanent black marker. I could see them as they once were: a declaration of a poor boy's heart to an unsuspecting girl, a sign of his love for her and for all of the rest of the school to see. I counted the cinderblocks from the bottom to the top. It was neat how the letters stood out from the wall, ancient. Maybe they were etched twenty years ago, and maybe that couple was married now with a family, and somehow, their love still remained a fixed part of our school hallway. I considered etching Rachel's name on the tree outside near the parking lot where some of my friends liked to hang and smoke cigarettes between classes.

I looked down at my long legs spread out before me on the checkered hallway floor. My sneakers were worn and scuffed in all the right places. My everyday wardrobe was basic: jeans, kicks, and a T-shirt. My mother was right: I was growing like a weed, taller than most of my classmates now. The hallway floor was chilly on my legs and the locker I leaned against smelled like metal. The final bell had rung and the parade of buses were leaving, my last chance for a ride home dissipating quickly.

Alex was late again.

I squeezed a tennis ball in my hand and inspected it. Somehow I knew that this ball would come in handy. I bounced the ball on the floor, watching it land squarely on the cinderblock next to the one with the scribbled black faded initials.

"Shit! So close!"

The ball bounced back and I caught it. I stared at the yellowed object. Feeling confident, I threw it against the ground one more time.

The hallway was empty. I could hear slight murmurs of teachers, but I couldn't see them. They were probably talking about how awful their day was, how the little twelfth grade kids were some of the worst class of punks they had ever taught.

I hit my target. The ball landed on the ground, making an empty sound as it bounced and rolled toward my feet. I could almost hear the squeal of Rachel's tennis shoes as she would run for the return serve, her arm stretched eloquently in a backswing. This was Rachel's tennis ball. I had every intention of returning it to her tomorrow, full of the opportunity I now had to speak with her, using the tennis ball as an excuse.

I found her beautiful. Rachel's hair was a silky wave of dark brown curl, long down her back. She mostly wore tennis skirts and tennis shoes but sometimes she dressed like me: sneakers, jeans, and a T-shirt.

Rachel, she was special.

I could hear footsteps now, echoing down the hallway. I looked up to see Mrs. Maloney, the school's head secretary. She was glancing down at me as if sitting on the ground was some sort of crime.

"William, your mom called. She sounded confused. She said she needed you to come home, so I told her I would see if I could find you."

I tried not to look annoyed.

"You could still make the late bus if you want to," she went on. "It's about ready to leave so I would hurry if I were you."

I glanced up at her. "Alex said he would pick me up but I guess he forgot." I bounced off the floor to my feet, grabbed my backpack and swung it over my shoulder. "I better go now. Thank you, Mrs. Maloney."

12

It was embarrassing, the way my mom would call the school sometimes. I felt heavy thinking about it, unsure what it was I would be coming home to. I watched Mrs. Maloney walk away, my mind filled with everything that seemed to be cascading down on me at once. No one understood my situation like Alex. He was my best friend and since I only had one, he was very important to me.

As I thought about my mom's multitude of health issues, it occurred to me that without Alex, my life would consist of me sitting in my bedroom listening to music and handing out daily anti-depression medication to my mother, which made having a personal life sometimes difficult. Alex often saved me from my own sadness, which is what friends do, if you're lucky.

I continued down the hallway and exited the building's main entrance, my head cloudy with thoughts. As I moved forward, a dragonfly buzzed around me. I stopped and stood quietly, unmoving, and let it land on my shoulder. Its colors were vivid—bright purples and greens—and it too seemed to stop moving, as if we were one. It was odd how it appeared. I had never seen a dragonfly this close before, and was surprised at how it seemed to greet me so unexpectedly.

I watched it fly away, and just like that it was gone.

I started walking again, thinking about Rachel, the girl of my dreams. Nothing could upset me today, because of the opportunity I'd take tomorrow. I still held the tennis ball in my hand. It was the perfect chance to overcome my fear and approach her.

I smiled and walked toward the bus.

I promised myself: Tomorrow I would speak to her.

Tomorrow I would be brave.

Chapter

Two

When the bus dropped me off, I walked across the street to the house I grew up in, the house where I lived with my mother. The small two-bedroom wasn't much to look at but I took care of it the best I could. We had a small yard that I mowed every week and a short picket fence that bordered my neighbor's driveway.

Two police cars were parked along the front sidewalk, which wasn't unusual. The cops regularly visited the couple who lived next door, John and Carol. The neighbors' struggle with drugs and alcohol was evident in the way they ignored their littered property, and the broken-down fencing and piles of junk. Weeds lined the foundation of the house along with grass that grew, but was never cut. Their children's playthings were scattered all over the backyard, broken toys that needed to be tossed and clothing left to deteriorate wherever it may land.

It was my mother's favorite pastime to stare out of our living room window, taking note of all the activity going on at the house next door. Sometimes my mother watched just to keep an eye on the children who were always outside, unsupervised.

Stalling, I moved up the walkway, listening to my neighbor Carol argue with one of the police officers. I shook my head, feeling sorry for the poor man. Carol wasn't what you'd call college educated. It's possible that she graduated from high school, but I doubted it. When she spoke, she sounded unintelligent, even though she wasn't. Actually, she was quite bright when you caught her in a normal state of mind.

As I listened to her speak, I wanted to scream at her, "The officer wasn't born yesterday, Carol! It's obvious your children haven't been bathed in a while." But I didn't. I kept to myself.

Carol's boyfriend John had a knack for drama. He came flying out of the house, his big mouth moving quickly. He approached the police office with aggression, as if he were someone they should fear.

"She's done nothing wrong, goddamn it! Do you have some kind of warrant, Officer, to be interrogating her like this?" John confronted the officer so rapidly that the officer stepped back and drew his gun.

16

"Hold it right there! Don't move another foot and put your hands up in the air."

Now this is interesting. I lingered along the sidewalk, pretending to pick up small wooden debris that had fallen from the oak tree in our front yard.

John put his hands up in the air and seemed startled by the officer's hostile stance. "Oh man, I just wanted to talk to you. This is some kind of bullshit, you pulling a gun on me."

Carol stepped toward John and tried to console him. "Just stay calm baby, everything is a big misunderstanding."

"Get the fuck away from me." John shrugged Carol away from his arm. "Be useful and go call my lawyer," he yelled at her.

I chuckled under my breath. *He doesn't have a dime to his name but he has a lawyer on call?* He probably needed a lawyer more than once or twice in his life. His guy was probably one of those billboard lawyers whose picture wasn't really the guy, but some stand-in actor who was more handsome and photogenic.

Another police car pulled up and the officer got out of his vehicle. I nodded my head toward him and said, "Good afternoon, sir." The officer pulled John aside and walked him toward the curb while the other officer engaged Carol. I rolled my eyes. What a waste of our community's resources, to be spending time with those two.

I continued up the sidewalk when a woman caught my eye. I hadn't noticed her before, but she was standing at the fence, watching me. Her hair was long, braided down her back and a heavy sweater was wrapped around her shoulders and arms. Her smile revealed a few missing teeth, but her eyes were green and warm; her face was round and full of color.

She pointed her finger at me then beckoned me closer. I hesitated, figuring she was a friend of Carol's and probably had some interesting backstory that led to John and Carol's most recent police encounter.

I walked closer, reluctant. She held my attention, just by her sheer appearance, but she was startling to look at. She was unique, even down to the jewelry she wore, which was something I had never seen before. Large stones and crystals draped around her neck and she smelled like smoke mixed with lavender.

I waited for her to speak. She glared into my face and I watched her eyes roll backward into her head. The whites of them became prevalent and I could no longer see her pupils.

My eyes widened. Something strange was happening.

"Do you believe in magic?" she asked. Her voice was crisp, but her tone was much different than what I expected. Her voice was feminine, even though she appeared rugged and abused, as if some sort of hard life had befallen her. I think the confusion on my face forced her to continue.

"You're too busy to believe in magic, aren't you?"

I was still confused, but nodded.

"Carol and John, they make bad decisions for themselves."

I laughed. "That's an understatement."

"Yes, it is." The woman gestured toward the police car. "It's like a game of chess," she started. "If you make the wrong move, the game can be over."

I narrowed my eyes onto her face. I wasn't sure what she was talking about, but she had my attention.

"You know, Will, we all have choices to make in this lifetime. Each choice you make can unlock a piece of the grid and can either elevate you to the next level or it can hinder you and keep you back."

"How did you know my name?" I asked.

"There's danger in your life, Will. You need to pay attention. You need to make sure you unlock the proper boxes and move forward, or you may be putting your life at risk."

"What are you talking about?" I asked. She wasn't making any sense.

"Your mother too. Her grid is congested."

I was getting irritated. "What the fuck is a grid?"

"A grid is your life path. When you unlock certain pieces or boxes of your grid, you expose new and exciting elements to your life. Boxes can unlock when you make good choices for yourself, and through positivity, you can expand and grow as a person. The same is the opposite when you make poor choices for yourself: The boxes can close." She paused. "You're mother doesn't want to live. Maybe now she's okay, but she's difficult and I can feel that."

"My mother has problems," I agreed because she was right. My mother didn't want to live at times. Her depression was so bad that at one point, I was afraid that she would kill herself while I was at school. There were days when she never left her bed other than to use the bathroom, and food was a real issue for her. She hated to eat, never felt famished or motivated by hunger pains. In the past I had been forced to beg her to take small bites, because I was afraid they'd put her in the hospital again.

"You'll be facing many crossroads. Choose wisely, Will. Your life will depend on it."

All I could picture was a video game I used to play, whose main objective was to follow the right path and make the right moves through the maze, all the while being chased by demons and faced with obstacles. As I would unlock the codes, more doors would open and I would advance to the next level. It took me a long time to reach the end of that game, and as I progressed through it, the levels became more challenging and the choices I needed to make were less clear. I spent months playing that game. I was determined to make it through to the end and win.

Goosebumps ran up my arms and all through my body. My hands were sweaty and her words unsettled me. I turned to walk away, feeling unease and irritated, thinking she was just a friend of Carol's. She was a nobody. I decided to pay her no mind.

"Follow your instincts, Will," she yelled one last time.

"Yeah, okay then, thank you," I mumbled. "Have a good day ma'am." *Crazy lady.* I waved her off and walked up the steps to my front porch.

An empty dog crate sat near the door, the one I used when I brought home my dog Molly from the pet store. It was a miserable feeling at times, coming home knowing that she wasn't there. When I would think about her, I got a sinking feeling, or like getting the wind knocked out of me. It was hopeless, trying to find her. I spent weeks looking when she went missing. I posted signs and walked house to house in our neighborhood, hoping someone might have seen her, seen *something*.

My mother went silent whenever I tried to talk to her about it. *She* was the reason Molly was gone. She let her out of the house and Molly never came back. Perhaps she felt terrible about the incident, but she would never acknowledge it. She acted like it never happened, as if Molly never existed. I'm not even sure if my mother understood.

I loved animals. Animals give unconditionally, and their love is pure. It was the first time in my life I felt love like that, it was so easy with her. I wanted to get another dog but my mother was adamantly against it, and even though I knew a new dog could never replace Molly, a new dog could at least ease the pain of losing her, just a little. Plus, my mother needed the dog's attention more than I did. She needed the companionship. But I couldn't explain that to her. She couldn't understand.

My mother. She was what you called bipolar, although she was never formally diagnosed. For years, doctors placed her on certain levels of anti-anxiety and anti-depression medications, which only seemed to disable her more. On top of that, my mother was an alcoholic. This was the big secret between us, although I suspected that my aunt Bev knew of my mother's behaviors. Mom had forbidden me to talk about it with anyone else, including the doctors and especially my father.

My mother's name was Linda and I would call her that at times just to piss her off. *Linda* was very good at being unhealthy mentally and physically, yet I did my best to cover for her, defend her, and protect her. I never really knew who I was coming home to or what frame of mind she would be in. Some days she was the greatest person to be around. She had energy, excitement in her voice, and God, I really thought she could be capable of anything. Other days, she could get lost into a dark place within her mind and it would be difficult to pull her out. When I was younger, this type of exchange confused me.

Still, I took care of her. I tried to make life easier for us.

My book bag slid to the floor as I tossed my jacket over the coat rack. "Hey Mom!"

"Oh. Oh. William, you're home. Good...good...good. I need you to do something for me. I need you to come here and take a look through these and tell me what you see. I've been trying to figure this out all day, but I can't. I just can't. I think I need new glasses or something because I just can't figure out what's on that table out there in the neighbors' yard. Is that a real bird, or is that a statue? COME HERE PLEASE! Take a look at this for me."

My mother was standing exactly in the same place that she stood every day, next to the window, staring at the neighbors' yard. It was always so abrupt when I came home; she instantly wanted my attention the minute I walked through the front door. It was exhausting.

"I'm starving, Mom!"

I could smell the reek of wine on her breath, and her stance was off balanced. She held on to the wall, leaning toward the window. "Never mind about that, just look at this." My mother pulled me toward the window and handed me her trusty binoculars. I took a deep breath and stared through the cloudy lenses. A few seconds of my time would appease her. I straightened up and handed back her binoculars.

"It's a statue, Mom. It's not going to move."

My mother withdrew from me and squinted, her face suddenly stern and unwavering.

"Well that's just stupid. Why do they have a statue of a bird on their table?"

I started to walk toward my bedroom. "I don't know, Linda!" I yelled from the hallway.

"Wait, Will. Wait. I need to talk to you."

I paused before opening my bedroom door. "What is it?" I asked, frustrated. "Is it about the police officers? Because I've already spoken to them and they say they'll be leaving soon. Seems like they have everything under control."

"No, no, that's fine. They've been here all day. It's something else. I've been thinking about this and I really think I have a good chance." My mother started to pace back and forth over the living room carpet.

"A good chance for what, Mom?"

"It's just a really good chance. I spoke to the manager, and she said so. She said I have a really good chance to get the job."

I inhaled deeply, as deep as I could manage, and counted to ten. She'd get like this; it was a part of her problem. Her energy levels went up and down and her mind worked overtime—the ideas, the obsessions with things. It was hard for her to balance these moods she'd get into. My mother hadn't worked in years; she was incapable of working and in fact she was on disability because of her illness.

"Mom, listen to me." I held on to her hands. "I'm glad you have a chance. I wish you the best with that. I hope you get it, the job."

My mother took a few steps backward and looked at me. She paused, her eyes darting across my face as if she wasn't sure how to react to my positive reinforcement. Maybe I offended her with my disinterest in having a confrontation with her today. Maybe it was the alcohol she drank, but her face was still and she wavered where she stood, as if she didn't know which direction to move.

When I was young, my mother worked for a while. It didn't last; she could never hold a job for very long. She was inconsistent, calling out regularly whenever she felt overwhelmed or depressed. We struggled financially for years, until my aunt helped us apply for disability. After that, things seemed okay. I knew that we could at least count on that check, and I worked hard to supplement any money that I could. I mowed lawns and did small clean-up jobs for some of our neighbors. In the winter, I would shovel sidewalks and driveways, just to have a little extra money.

I thought about the gypsy woman's warning about the boxes and how my mother didn't want to live at times.

My mother suffered trauma as a young child. My great grandparents raised her and Aunt Bev after my mother's mother was killed in a tragic car accident. A baby brother also died in the crash. My mother was ten years old then, old enough to remember the horror of it and to understand that her grandparents weren't kind people. They blamed my mother and aunt for the car crash. Because they were undisciplined children, my great grandparents said Linda and Bev were a distraction to my grandmother's driving, which caused her to lose control of her vehicle.

My mother didn't remember it that way. It was raining hard the moment of the crash, my mother told me once, and the road was filled with large pools of water. She remembered the car losing control and hitting the edge of a construction barrier.

When my mother would drink, she talked about the abuse she endured after she moved in with her grandparents. Her grandfather made them work on the farm from early morning until late at night, without any breaks or lunch. If they misbehaved, he would beat them with a horsewhip until their legs bled. Sometimes she would cry, talking about how she missed her mother and lost the beautiful life she should have had.

I tried to reason with her, always believing that life is what you make of it. I tried to pull her out of her depressive thoughts by keeping things lighthearted and making jokes. If I could make her laugh at herself for a good fifteen minutes, it was really helpful.

"Mom!" My tone of voice startled her out of her trance and she focused on me. I realized I only had a few seconds of her attention. "Let's move the bird!" If I knew anything about my mother, I knew that causing Carol a little bit of mischief was right up her alley. "Come on, it will be fun and we won't get caught, I promise."

The edges of my mother's mouth rose slightly but her eyes narrowed. "Are you sure it's not real?" she asked suspiciously.

"It's not. Let's go quickly, before we get caught."

My mother went and stood by the window again. "I don't see anyone, Will. I think it's a good time; no one's outside. What are you going to do with it?"

I glanced outside the back door and perused Carol's yard. She had a basket on her porch, which she filled daily with damp laundry for the clothesline.

"I'm going to place it in the basket, so when she opens it to hang her laundry the bird will be there, staring at her and will probably scare the hell out of her."

My mother's eyes gleamed and her face was wide with pleasure. "Oh Will!" Her laugh was priceless and I loved so much when I heard it.

"I'll be right back, Mom. Keep a look-out." I left the house and crouched around the fence toward the picnic table. *The things I do for my mother.* I was proud of my ability to play practical jokes on people, and especially proud of how fast I was when I needed to be.

I grabbed the owl and tiptoed onto Carol's deck, putting the bird inside the basket, then sprinted back to my house, all within thirty seconds. Laughing, I had to admit the excitement was good for me too.

When I returned to my mother, I could see the worry still lingering in her eyes.

"What if the bird flies away?" she asked.

I put my arm around her gently. She was a good mother; for years she took care of me. I led her to the couch and sat her down. "It won't Mom, I'm sure of it."

It didn't always last long, the joy, but I always tried, and sometimes it worked.

The stillness in the room was familiar, the sudden quietness that struck me with guilt. I kissed her on the head and turned the TV on for her. She looked up at me with scared eyes. These were the moments I wished we still had our dog. Molly would jump on the couch with her and lay down in her lap. My mother would look down at her and pet her. Molly would snap her right out of her moment of silence.

I could see my mother was trying to put it all together in her mind, but it was overwhelming her.

"Mom, how about a cup of tea?"

My mother's eyes lit up. "Yes! Yes, William. Thank you. A cup of tea."

I covered her with a blanket and walked into the kitchen.

My mother needed me.

She needed me, and I needed to get a dog.

Chapter
Three

My classes kept me busy the next day. At lunch, I sat down in my usual spot and waited for Alex to join me. My phone was vibrating, messages coming in from a group text about friends getting together after the football game. I ignored the calls. Friday night was on everyone's minds, especially mine.

The varsity football game was a big deal in our town since we played our biggest rivalry, The Warriors. The football jocks would be walking the school hallways dressed in their shirts and ties, and the faculty wore their favorite team jerseys in show of support.

Alex was across the room, talking to the girls at the freshmen table.

He was my social hero. He was everything I was not and had the confidence of a male underwear model, and the girls thought he looked like one too. I met Alex when we were eight years old and I remember it, clearly still. We were at a convenience store, a block away from my house. My mother needed groceries, so I walked there with ten dollars in my pocket. I thought about what I would buy, if there was any change left over. Pop Rocks, because of the way they made my mouth feel.

Alex was scrawny then and he held tightly to a water gun in one hand, his mother's hand in the other. I asked to look at it. It was fluorescent green and showed promises of accurate and distant spraying. The gun fit my hand perfectly but as I looked down at the basket of groceries I held, I realized that I wouldn't be able to buy it.

"Hello," Alex's mom said. "What's your name?" she asked.

"My name is William."

"William, this is Alex. Do you two know each other?" she asked.

Alex smiled at me and grabbed his water gun right out of my hand. "There's another one, over there." He pointed.

I nodded but then continued to walk toward the cashier.

"Well, aren't you going to get one?" Alex asked. He finally let go of his mother's hand and came to stand next to me.

"I can't. I don't have enough money."

"Can't you ask your mom for money?"

"She gave me ten dollars, but I have to buy these groceries with it."

I was careful not to say more. Alex's mom was staring at me and I had the sense that going to a convenience store alone as an eight-year-old was probably something Alex never did. Alex looked up at his mom with a small spark in his eye.

"Mom?"

Alex's mom smiled. "Yeah, okay. Grab another gun."

I dropped my groceries and we both ran to the shelf and debated over which color I should get. I grabbed the light blue one and then we stumbled and shoved our way toward the gas station bathroom to fill them up. Alex's mom waited patiently in the parking lot as we shot at each other around her car, hiding and ducking, laughing. We'd been best friends ever since.

Alex's mom put my groceries in her car and drove me home that day. She watched me as I walked up the sidewalk, a knowing look in her eye and concern for me. Perhaps it was the broken-down fencing surrounding our property, or the fact that I was grocery shopping alone. Perhaps it was the look I gave her when she asked me about my mother. Either way, I think she understood that I was growing up much different than Alex.

Alex was an only child, and so was I. Over time, his mother had persuaded mine to allow me to stay with them on occasion, and to do things with them, like go to the movies or swim at the local town pool, which was one of our favorite pastimes. She even had an extra bike at her house so that when I came, we could cruise the streets together, just Alex and me. He was spoiled with love; he didn't know how lucky he was. Both his parents adored him, and so did every girl at our school.

I worried about him, though. I was used to disappointment. I learned to accept that my life wasn't perfect, but Alex's life seemed perfect in every way. It was fun to watch him react when things didn't quite go his way.

He glanced up at me as he came and sat down at the table, his eyes heavy.

"What's wrong buddy?" I asked. "Not enough phone numbers this time?"

Alex had a problem with dating. He was what the girls called a player, constantly needing attention from someone. I think he was overly loved sometimes, because one girl was never enough for him. Still, I was envious. He had a way with them and a confidence that I lacked in every way.

"What's the plan tonight? Are we going to the game?" he asked, ignoring my question.

Distracted, I looked past Alex and watched as Rachel sat down at the table behind him. "I was planning on it," I replied.

"Good. I'll pick you up around 6:00."

"Yeah, okay, that's cool."

"What are you staring at?" Alex turned around to look at the table behind him. "Oh, never mind, tough guy. Are you going to talk to her, or just stare at her?" He waited for my reply but I was lost in my focus. "The girls are always talking about that creepy custodian who lingers around the second floor bathrooms. He's always staring at them. I'd like to beat that guy up."

I finally glanced at Alex.

"Don't be like the custodian." Alex grinned, knowing that statement would get under my skin.

I stood up from my seat. I looked at Alex for a brief moment and thought to myself, *Now's a good time to open a box.* Everything the gypsy said to me, I remembered. *I'm definitely not like the school custodian.*

"I wonder if she'll be at the game tonight," I spoke softly. *Maybe she'll drink a beer with me at an after party.*

Maybe I could make her laugh at herself…maybe I could kiss her. Thoughts swarmed my head as I stood still, wishing I were as charming as Alex. I didn't know what it was with Rachel, but she kept me frozen. Everything about her scared me.

I had promised myself this time that I would talk to her and return to her the tennis ball. Determined to be brave, I took my tray off the table and moved from the seat.

I faltered along the table where she sat, my heart pounding. She lifted her head and smiled. I smiled back. But then, my hands were sweating, my head felt flush as a wave of heat flooded my entire body. The whole cafeteria was watching me make a fool of myself. I continued walking past her, and tightly closed my eyes. I knew how I felt and I just wasn't ready. My words would have appeared nervous because I was, and that's not how I wanted it to go down.

My phone vibrated and I glanced down at the message.

Pussy! Alex wrote.

I turned around, smiled, and gave him the finger.

I laughed at myself. I was a pussy.

The opportunity to talk to Rachel was perfect, and I let it slip right through my fingers. She probably thought I was crazy, just standing there staring at her.

Fuck.

She was probably right anyway.

Chapter

Four

Later that night, Alex called me; his tone was something I'd never heard from him before. He asked if he could pick me up because he needed to talk. I wasn't sure what to expect, but Alex was my best friend and he needed me.

When he came, we drove around the neighborhood, finding a quiet place to park. He lit up a joint and passed it to me with this stressed look over his face, as though he'd just seen a ghost.

"What's up?" I asked as I settled into the seat, feeling much more relaxed than before.

"Something fucked up just happened, and I don't even know what to think about it."

Alex tapped on the speed shift, his face vulnerable while he shook his head in tiny little jolts.

"I can tell you're freaking out. Relax a little, so we can figure this out. It can't be that big of a deal, Alex. What happened?"

Alex took a deep breath. "I came home early from school today, like I always do, fucking hungry."

A car drove by and Alex stopped talking until it passed.

"I made a sandwich and then noticed a fresh bushel of white tulips on the counter, Mom's favorite, along with a small package wrapped with brown paper and silk ribbon. There was a hand-written card next to the package."

Alex reached into his pocket and removed the note and handed it to me.

Elizabeth, all my love and thoughts are with you, always. xo

I stared at Alex as he spoke. I could see the confusion all over his expression as he gripped the steering wheel, the bags under his eyes dark. I wasn't sure if I should be asking questions or where he was heading with this story, so I sat still and listened, knowing that whatever he was going to share was important.

"My father wasn't home, but I've never seen him bring Mom flowers anyway. It wasn't his style. He'd rather just hand her cash and tell her to go buy what she needed."

Thoughts were racing through my mind. I was putting the pieces together.

"I got a real uneasy feeling that maybe I came home a little too early today. My mother was home—I could tell because her car was in the garage and her purse was on the counter. The only place she could've been was in her bedroom. I thought about making some loud noise to bring attention to myself. I thought about turning on the music and screaming her name, just to announce my presence, and then locking myself inside my bedroom and pretending I didn't know what was going on."

"Yeah…" I nodded. "That would have been a good idea." I spoke softly, feeling anxious over what Alex was about to tell me. *It couldn't possibly be.* His mother had been acting strange for months now. Alex had mentioned this but thought maybe she was going through a mid-life crisis or something. She had been unexplainably happy but distant too, and spending time with her girlfriends, especially the neighbor Angie, his mother's best friend. My heart was still and reluctant to know what the truth of it was. I wasn't sure I wanted to know this, but Alex needed me.

"I finished my sandwich and walked toward my bedroom. I kept thinking, *I don't want to know* over and over in my mind, as I went up the staircase." Alex bit his lip and I thought he was going to make himself bleed, his face so tortured. "Mom's bedroom door was closed. I could hear voices coming from her room, and my heart sank. I stood and listened more closely, realizing that they were female voices."

"Oh." I straightened up. I felt relief flood through me as I realized that it was just his mother and her friend, probably Angie, doing whatever women do behind closed doors. They were probably looking at the curtains and rearranging furniture. I laughed at his stupidity and shook my head. But Alex was still so serious.

"So, I walked down the hallway and knocked on the door while opening it. Mom sat on her bed in her nightgown. She stood up and grabbed her bathrobe, real nervous like."

Alex swallowed hard and closed his eyes.

"I looked around the bedroom and saw no one, but I knew I heard voices. I asked her who she was talking to, but she was eager to push me out of her room…but she wasn't strong enough to force me out. I heard the voice again and Angie came out of the master bathroom." Alex turned to me and grabbed my shoulder. "You should have seen her face," he explained. "She must've used the shower because she had nothing on but a towel."

I hadn't moved since Alex started talking. I didn't know if it was the weed or Alex's story, but I was motionless. I seemed to stop breathing, anticipating every word he was saying. My body felt stiff and rigid, shocked at what Alex was insinuating about his mother.

"My mother made some excuse about Angie's plumbing and finally shut the door on me, promising she'd come and talk to me shortly. I didn't want to speculate, but something wasn't right. It was 12:30 in the afternoon; this didn't make sense to me. I thought about the look on my mother and Angie's face, like they had been caught or something. Maybe she was having an affair with Angie."

"Wow Alex, are you sure about that? Maybe you misunderstood."

Alex raised his eyebrows at me and continued. "I heard my mother's door open and anticipated her walking into the kitchen."

Alex and his mother were always very close. His father worked long days and since Alex was an only child, he and his mother spent countless hours together. His mother was one of the most kind and caring women I had ever known. She treated me as if I were family and always showed love for Alex, even when he was acting like a jerk. They had a close and trusting relationship. I was sure Alex wouldn't want that to change. He wouldn't want her to feel alienated or unable to communicate with him, considering that this was a big conversation to have. I could tell his feelings were complicated and conflicted; he really didn't understand what was happening.

"My mother and Angie finally came downstairs, awkward and uncomfortably making small talk with me. Angie left and my mother came back into the kitchen. I asked her what was going on. I asked her about the flowers and the gift and card."

"What did she say?" *Oh God.*

"She said I would never understand and that it was difficult to explain."

"Explain what? What was there to explain?" I asked.

"She said that she and Angie…they love each other. " Alex continued to stare, not knowing what to say next or how to react.

"She said she was in love with Angie?" My mouth fell open.

"Everything I ever understood about my mother changed in that moment, and there was nothing I could do to stop it. Mom started to cry. She said she was sorry." Alex stopped talking. His eyes were moist and I could tell he was still in shock.

"Holy shit Alex, this is crazy." I couldn't believe what he was telling me.

"She said she didn't know if she was gay and that it had nothing to do with being gay or being straight. It's as if Angie being a woman had no importance to her— she loved her; they had a strong connection that went far beyond that of their gender identity. She said it was spiritual between them, a natural bond that she didn't want to break."

"She's never been interested in women?"

"She claims never."

"So she's bisexual then?"

"I asked her the same thing. She said she just knows that Angie is her best friend and that she loves her unconditionally. She didn't know how they became attracted to each other sexually, but they did and it's been the most beautiful relationship she's ever had with someone. It felt real to her, like this was where she needed to be. She couldn't imagine her life without her."

I tried to get my mind around what Alex was saying.

"Now I have these horrible feelings, like what if I'm gay too, or could this ever happen to me?" Alex paused. "Could it?" He turned to me and was genuine in his question. I wanted to punch him in his arm.

"No, you fool. You're not gay, so stop it. It doesn't happen like that. It's weird that it happened to your mother in this way, but this must be a very unique situation."

Alex's face relaxed and he finally exhaled.

"What's she going to do about your father?" I asked.

Alex shook his head. "I have no idea. She needs to figure that out. Dad's not going to understand this. *I* don't even understand."

Sudden images of closing doors and boxes popped into my head and I thought about the gypsy lady on the fence. I hadn't mentioned it to Alex, because I wasn't sure how I felt about her. She said I was in danger, but that sort of comment seemed crazy to me.

"Hey Alex, can I ask you something?"

"Yeah, sure."

"Do you believe in magic?"

Alex rolled his eyes. "This isn't a time for practical jokes, Will."

"No, no, I'm sorry. Not that kind of magic. Like, the mystery of life, magic."

"I hadn't really thought about it."

"I had this conversation with a gypsy woman the other day, and she warned me about my life. About making choices and unlocking boxes to further advance my life's path. Something like that."

Alex nodded. "That seems weird. When did you run into a gypsy lady?"

"She was at the neighbors'."

"Oh, figures. Forget it, man. Anyone willing to hang out with your neighbors is sure to be a little bit crazy."

Most of my friends knew about my neighbors. It was always a good subject of conversation. "So anyway, she was really unnerving. I've been looking for her ever since and she hasn't come back around. I almost feel like I've imagined her."

"What does that mean, unlocking boxes?"

"It's like with Rachel: I can choose to sit back and do nothing with regards to my feelings for her, or I can unlock the box, not knowing what will happen, but take the risk anyway and talk to her, tell her how I feel. She scares me, but now I feel like it's important to face her, to overcome my fears around girls." I laughed at myself. There really wasn't much to be nervous about. It was all in my head.

"Oh, I get it. I can relate that with my mother. She's definitely unlocking some boxes. That's actually a helpful way to look at things. It's scary, though, to follow a path that you're unsure of. She's going through some things right now, and making some big choices for her life. It's like, *so big* and I'm not sure how we're all going to make it through it."

I looked at him and felt his sadness. His parents had saved me in a lot of ways. They gave me experiences that I would not have had otherwise, from my own parents. "I know it has something to do with fear, unlocking boxes. She mentioned my mother too. My mother has always been afraid."

"It sounds like you should be facing challenges as opposed to running from them. You need to take some risks in order to enjoy the reward."

"Yeah, maybe you're right about that." We both sat in silence and in thought about what was going on in our lives. "I think that your family is really strong and no matter what happens with your mother and father, they love you and you need to support them and love them too. It's the only way you'll get through this—with love for them."

"I think you're right about that, Will. It's going to be a weird adjustment, but I can muddle through it until it feels right. Someday this may all feel very normal to me. I always liked Angie. I can see why my mother loves her."

Alex had an open and caring heart, he always had. He was always positive about things, even when they were difficult.

"You got this, buddy," I stated and he smiled as we bumped our fists together.

"To opening boxes."

Chapter

Five

After Mom's behavior yesterday and Alex's revelation about his mother, I was looking forward to a night out with my friends. My mother was still on my mind when Alex and I arrived at the high school football game. I hated leaving her alone at night, but I had to live a life. I called Aunt Bev to come and stay with her but she had already made plans. Bev was a short, plump woman who loved to wear those crock style shoes, the kind nurses always wore with her bell-bottom jeans and a flannel shirt with a vest. She worked hard and led a tough love type of ship. Still, she never seemed available when I needed her.

Alex drove an old Chevy Impala his father gifted him when he turned sixteen. It was cool because the back seat was wide and could hold a lot of friends, and besides that, it really gained status and attention from our classmates. No matter where we went, people stared. The passenger door was always difficult to open, though. I had to gear up my strength and push the heavy metal forcibly but controllably, so I could exit the vehicle and not look like such a jerk in doing so.

"When are you going to fix this shit, Alex?"

"It's part of her charm," Alex replied as he rubbed the dashboard lovingly.

I laughed. "Yeah, she's got charm all right."

Alex smirked sideways at me.

"Let's just say you're jealous and we'll leave it at that."

He was right. I was very envious of his car and his methods. I didn't have nearly enough confidence to do the things Alex did. I wanted to learn, though; I'd been told that's half the battle.

We parked in the far south corner of the parking lot, the football field a mile away. It was where all the kids parked. Friday night tailgating was still allowed at our school, but in other schools, the faculty was starting to shut it down and restrict areas where the students could hang out together. Last week a student was killed in a car accident after a football game at Century Hills High School, a few towns over. The student had been drinking at the game and drove himself right across the highway and hit a tree. You could still see the flowers and crosses that were placed along the road in memory of him. It was only a matter of time they would crack down on us too.

It didn't matter tonight. We were smart about what we did, anyway. We were safe.

Alex walked around to the trunk of his car and opened it; inside were two large red coolers perched in the back. I encouraged him with my smile and helped myself to a nice cold beer. Alex cracked open a bottle of Fireball. "Cheers!" he said as we clinked our bottles together.

I could feel the worry and stress over my mother start to dissipate. I had this relentless guilt when it came to her. She was always in my thoughts, like an endless parade of comments that sat with me. *"When will you be home, William? What if I get hurt? I'm all alone again!"* She didn't realize how exhausting those comments could be, as if I were solely responsible for any source of happiness that she may be grasping at.

The alcohol squashed those thoughts. It drowned out the noise, helping my shoulders relax; the voices of my friends and classmates calmed me. We would drink and smoke pot on occasion, but everything in moderation, as my mother once said. She was talking about the neighbors' excessive use of their electricity, but I took what I wanted from that conversation. I applied it to my own life.

Alex nudged my arm. "Hey, how was your mom tonight, when you left her?"

"The usual. Feeling sorry for herself that I was going out."

Alex looked at me long and his tone became soft and serious. "She'll be all right, Will. She's got you, and besides, she never ever leaves the house. She'll be home waiting for you like she always does. She'll be fine." Alex opened another beer and handed me the bottle.

"Any more success with Rachel? Have you redeemed yourself from punking out at lunch the other day?" Alex's sideways glance reminded me of how stupid that was.

I took the bottle and exhaled a deep breath. "I wasn't thinking of Rachel, but now that you mention her, I wonder where she is tonight."

"She'll be here with her friends. I'm sure of it." Alex leaned against the car close to me as we looked out across the parking lot. Cars were starting to pull in and a few more of our friends had arrived.

I closed my eyes. It was no use worrying about my problems. When I opened them, the sunrays had spread beneath the clouds, casting bright shades of pink and purple across the sky. I thought about how beautiful it was, the sunset. I imagined Rachel and I sitting together, watching the sun settle for the night, holding her hand. I imagined that maybe we could lay together then and watch darkness fall. We could watch the moonrise and the stars in the sky, just lay there, me holding her hand and listening to her breathe.

Alex jeered me with his elbow, right in my rib.

"Christina's cheering tonight," he mentioned. "She says she might be around afterward, but no promises. I swear, this girl drives me absolutely crazy!"

I started to rub my side as I let go of my daydream. "You play too many games with her. She knows you like her but you have too many girlfriends. She's not into it."

"Ohhh, maybe I should start acting like you then. Maybe I should ignore her and stare at her from behind my locker."

I jumped off the trunk of the car. "Fuck you Alex. I'm just trying to help. Do what you want, it's your life."

His comment stung, but he was right. I needed to stop playing around and have more confidence. *Easier said than done.* I wish I wasn't so afraid of what Rachel thought of me. It kept me from talking to her; I valued her opinion so much. I couldn't risk the rejection. I'd rather obsess over her secretly than know the truth of it.

53

My face must've looked hurt because Alex was quick to apologize. "Hey man, you know I'm just kidding around with you. Do what you need to do, it's no big deal." He put his arm around my neck and we walked toward the football field. "Stop worrying so much," he said. "Rachel will bring a smile to your face. Did I tell you that my mom had lunch with Rachel's mom the other day?"

"No, you didn't!" I shoved Alex lightly; he knew that I needed to know things about her. Any information was helpful.

"My mother can't stand Rachel's stepfather. He's a real piece of work, and Rachel, all she does is try to please him and make him happy. Rachel's mother seems clueless as to what goes on between them. She doesn't see anything wrong in their relationship."

I could relate to this—both our mothers were clueless. I think that's why I cared so much about her. She tried so hard and did amazing things for herself, but she had no idea how special she was. She could be really timid at times and shy socially, but when she spoke, she was so smart and intelligent. She was in all the advanced classes at school and she was an amazing tennis player. Not to mention how beautifully natural she was.

"Hey, remember she dated that guy Andrew in sophomore year?" I asked. "He broke up with her right in front of the nurse's office, I couldn't believe it. Why would *anyone* break up with her?"

"I think he was switching schools, if I remember correctly."

"I'll never forget her face. She wanted so desperately to change his mind."

"Yeah, I remember how down on herself she was afterward," Alex said, nodding. "He was so mean to her and she still wanted to be with him, badly."

"He was such an asshole." I paused. "I never told anyone this, but after that happened, I left Rachel an anonymous note in her locker. I told her how smart and wonderful she was and how strong I thought she was." Even then, I was afraid to approach her. "After that, she seemed better. She seemed to smile more and finally I think she got over him." I shook my head. I would have done anything to date Rachel. She and I were friends; we'd been in some of the same classes and had the same teachers since middle school. It was hard to understand why I felt this way toward her, other than my heart would race when I got next to her and when our eyes met, they would never waver. It was like we were having a silent love affair that neither of us was brave enough to bring to the surface.

I frowned at the thought of Rachel and her stepfather. It wasn't a secret that he was mean to her. I saw it myself at times, when he would come to the tennis matches. He would scream at her the entire match, never encouraging her with positivity, but criticizing her and how she performed. Then, when the match was over, he would retreat back to his car and wait for her, never smiling or saying a kind word to anyone.

"What else did your mom say?" I asked.

"Not that much." Alex's voice trailed off. Staring down at the ground, he looked lost in his thoughts.

"Any word about what happened the other day, with your mom and Angie?"

"No, but she and Dad went out to dinner tonight, to talk. I'm a little worried to know what I'll be coming home to later."

I raised an eyebrow at him. "You can always stay at my house," I offered.

Alex nodded. "Anyway, sorry about Rachel. Next time I'll ask more questions for you."

I put my arm around him. "Rachel's important to me, but you're important to me too. Is there something

I can help you with, something I can do for your mom? You know that I love her too. She's like my second mom, the good mom." I started to laugh, but it was true. She was my only normal gauge as to what real parenting should look like.

"Thanks, Will. I'm not sure what I need to do to help Mom yet. However, I do know that I want to hook up with Christina." Alex's mischievous smile always made me feel lucky to be his friend.

"I feel like your womanizing is getting worse, ever since your mom came out of the closet. It's not a contest, Alex. I wish you would settle down with one girl. Love someone for a change."

"You're so philosophical lately. Stop it."

"I know. Ever since the gypsy." I laughed.

"Anyway, I'm not gay."

"No one thinks you're gay, Alex. You don't have to prove this to people."

"I also really love women."

"All right then." I started to laugh. "Do what you want."

The National Anthem started to play over the loudspeakers and I assumed the varsity team was out on the football field. Alex and I headed to the stadium.

I was starting to feel really relaxed. It helped, with the anxiety, to be around my friends, drinking and socializing. Alex was especially important to me. He didn't realize it, but he helped me too.

Chapter

Six

The energy of the game was unmistakably contagious. I felt alive, and best of all, Rachel was sitting with a few friends just two benches in front of me. I watched as she cheered our players and interacted with her girlfriends. She had amazing dimples and her eyes lit up when she spoke. It was as if she carried this bright light with her, just like Alex. She didn't recognize what an impact she had on people. Mostly me. I could watch her all day, if it wasn't too weird. I didn't want to give her the impression that I was a creep, because I wasn't. I found her beautiful. It was just that simple for me.

After the game, I followed the sea of classmates out of the bleachers and toward the parking lot. I still had alcohol running through my veins, which gave me the courage to approach Rachel as we were walking out of the stadium entranceway.

It was now or never.

I thought about the box and how I had promised myself that I would be brave. All I needed to do was ask her. The worst thing that could happen was that she would say no. I'd had worse things happen to me, like the time I dove into the town pool and lost my bathing suit. That was pretty bad—not exactly *as* bad, but at least this would be less embarrassing.

I tapped her on her shoulder. When she turned around and looked at me, she smiled. "Hey Will!"

"Hey." I grinned back. "What are you and your friends up to? Hey Heather!" Rachel's best friend stood close to the exit doors, away from the crowded hallway.

"Where's your sidekick Alex?" she asked.

I turned to look to my right and noticed that he was gone. "Oh, he's probably down at the field looking for Christina." I looked back at Rachel and smiled. "Hey, we have a few beers back at the car, if you girls want to come hang out for a while?"

Rachel's face dropped in disappointment. "We don't drink, Will, but thanks anyway." She laughed nervously. Heather stepped forward.

"We dooo drink, that's a lie."

Rachel's face appeared rosy and uncertain. She looked down at her hands while she pretended to inspect her nail polish.

"You don't have to drink, it's okay," I backpedaled. "We could just hang out and listen to the music."

Rachel turned and looked at Heather. Heather shrugged.

"She's hoping that maybe Andrew will be here. There's been a rumor going around that he's home visiting from college."

Rachel looked back at me, her face somewhat torn. "This has nothing to do with Andrew. We'll think about it, Will. My stepfather's really strict about curfew and I have to be very careful sometimes not to get in trouble. I would really like to though, hang out, but maybe another time."

Heather made an annoyed face at me. "Her stepfather's a real controlling asshole. She never gets to do anything fun. Andrew's not worth her time either, but I can't seem to get through to her about these jerks in her life."

I smiled the best I could, feeling the blow to my stomach empty out into my throat. "It's no big deal. We're parked in the back of the lot if you change your mind. You can't miss us."

"Sounds good," Heather said as they began to disappear into the crowd.

I watched Rachel walk away. "Fuck" escaped my mouth in a whisper, but I had to remind myself that she didn't say no, so that was good. Maybe she still had feelings for Andrew after all, and used her stepfather as an excuse to let me off easy.

When I was twelve, I begged Rachel to help me with some silly math homework. It was a lousy excuse then to get next to her but she agreed and I went to her house for a tutoring session. I stood in the kitchen with a stupid notepad in my hand, watching Rachel rush around, gathering her school papers off the table and shoving them into her backpack. The dishes at the sink were soaking in detergent and the counters were cluttered with artwork and last quarter's projects. She said that she was hoping her stepfather would look at her pile of accomplishments.

They were still there, untouched, and it was getting close to 5:00. She was nervous that he would be home soon.

"Mom!" Rachel yelled into the other room. Rachel's mother was busy, neatening the living room and positioning the pillows in perfect order on the couch.

"What is it honey? Did you finish cleaning the kitchen? You know your stepdad doesn't like to come home to a mess. I hoped that you would have cleaned today while I was working. I didn't expect to come home to this, and now he's on the way and everything is a mess."

Rachel's mother's voice belied her irritation and she fidgeted around the living room, placing every little thing in its place. The room was in meticulous order; this was *his* room and where he sat. I looked around, not sure what else she could have done to make it appear more perfect.

"Mom, did you take a look at my artwork? I was just wondering if I should keep it or throw it away."

"Just toss it. It's taking up space and adding to the clutter."

"What about Ray?"

"I'm sure he saw it, honey."

Rachel rolled her eyes. "He didn't see it," she said quietly as she brushed past me on her way back to the kitchen. I felt helpless and foolish just standing there. I wasn't sure what all the fuss was about.

"Is there anything I can do to help you?" I offered. I noticed a broom in the corner and thought I better start sweeping, or we'd never get to study. I could tell Rachel was disappointed about her artwork.

"Maybe you should consider holding on to a few of your favorite pieces. Maybe you could frame one for your room. In fact, I would like to take one home with me, if you wouldn't mind."

She smiled finally and allowed me to pick through the pile. I picked a bright red painting of a barn and a goat on a hill, with a sunset in the background.

"I got an A-minus in the class, but my math grade needs improvement. It makes my stomach sick when I think about it," she mentioned.

I thought it was a weird thing to mention because I wasn't very good at math, but it never made my stomach hurt. In fact, I was grateful now that I needed the extra help, because I was spending time with Rachel.

Rachel grabbed the rest of her things and walked outside with an armful of her colorful paper and beautiful creations toward the garage. I followed her, watching as she momentarily struggled to open the garbage can and throw everything inside. I thought about how much time she must've spent and how it was all going to be sent to the landfill.

Her stepfather pulled into the driveway and my heart started to race. The energy of the household revolved around him, and I could feel that Rachel and her mother walked on eggshells. Rachel whispered to me, "The dirty dishes are still in the sink and the table isn't set." We couldn't move past him—he would consider that disrespectful, she told me—so we waited.

"Hello sir," she spoke politely.

"Hello," I added and nodded my head.

He looked irritated, but I'm pretty sure he always looked like that.

"Rachel." He motioned for us to walk in front of him. She led the way back into the house and we watched her mother scrambling at the sink, nervously. She turned around and faced her husband.

"Hey honey," she said sweetly. "How was your day, dear?" Rachel's mother walked toward him and kissed him gently on the cheek. He watched her suspiciously then sat down at the table and waited for her to get him his beer.

Rachel said they did the same thing every night, like clockwork. It felt so rigid and unnatural, the way they all interacted. Rachel's real father had left them when she was young.

"I was too young to remember him but I remember my mother crying and moving from place to place, trying to find him. Eventually, she met Ray and he's been taking care of us ever since I was three. My mother explained to me once that it was more important

65

to feel safe and secure—to have food and a nice place to sleep—than it was to feel loved."

Maybe her mother was right about that. Ray kept them safe.

It seemed like a heavy price to pay, however, and I felt bad for her.

That was years ago, but I never forgot it. I felt a connection with Rachel then and I still did today. We weren't growing up so perfect, her and I. She was sweet, she really tried her best at everything. She was a good person.

I took a deep breath and started to look around for Alex as I walked out into the parking lot, back toward the car. The side lot had better service and quieter reception, so I dialed my house number and listened as the phone rang.

"Hello," she answered, her voice slow and groggy.

"You sleeping, Mom?"

"William?"

"Yeah Mom, did I wake you?"

"I think I dozed off, honey. Are you okay?"

"Yeah, I felt bad leaving you alone tonight. I'm sorry if I woke you; I wanted to make sure you were okay."

"Just really sleepy. Had a busy day."

"Okay, Mom. I'll be home later. Get some rest."

"Will?"

"Yeah, Mom?"

"Do you think the owl moved yet?"

I closed my eyes tightly. "No, Mom, it's still there. It's fine where it is."

"Okay honey. Goodnight then."

"Good night, Mom."

I rolled my eyes. Fucking owl.

I hate fucking owls.

Chapter
Seven

My mother had always accused me of being a daydreamer. Especially when I was young, I would dream about having lots of friends and feeling free to live like other children, who enjoyed being kids and without the responsibility of their parents. I had dreams of a mother who was happy and who successfully navigated life with ease and love for me.

Ever since I spoke with the gypsy, my dreams were becoming more like nightmares. I would wake some mornings covered with sweat and filled with anxiety, my heart racing, trying to remember the dreams and their meanings.

I spent the entire Saturday in bed, feeling anxious about my life and where I was heading. I told my mother that I was sick and she inadvertently took that as a sign to mean that it was time to clean the house. All day, the vacuum cleaner ran. All day she came in and out of my room, dusting, picking up my clothes, making noise. She kept mentioning taking a trip and wanting to make sure the house was clean when she returned. I tried to tell her she wasn't going anywhere, we weren't taking a trip, but she continued on about it.

I just wanted quiet. I just wanted to be alone.

I thought about the dream I had. I remembered running through the woods, being chased by animals that were trying to give me messages. I kept going, putting my hands over my ears to block out what they were saying. I struggled, panting, to an enormous tree lying across the pathway. I reached for the branches, eager to pull myself up. On top of the tree were tiny little field mice, running from side to side, crossing over my hands and snipping at me, as if encouraging and helping me move forward. They wanted me to get to the top of the tree and climb over to reach the other side, but I had so many doubts. I wasn't strong enough to pull myself and my legs were too weak to climb.

In the distance, I could hear the gypsy woman speak to me. "Think positively. You are strong, you are capable of persevering and succeeding in all you do. Listen to the messages; follow your intuition and instincts. Don't be afraid."

The animals were screaming behind me; talking like humans, they warned me over and over again. The fox was there, telling me to trust myself and to be wary of the people around me. Mr. Turtle was slow to the tree but his voice was distinct and wise, his advice to take things slowly, to protect myself and to move at my own pace. The wolves lay leisurely in the space beneath the fallen tree, offering me confidence and pleading me to follow them down their path, promising me I'd never be alone, promising me guidance and support. The mice cheered and squeaked for me as I clung to the branches.

I was encouraged but darkness came through and the clouds began to thicken. Vines began to move around the tree and encircle my body, squeezing me tight and wrapping my hands until they turned blue. I watched as blood dripped down my fingers, landing in my eyes and clouding my sight. The loud wind was blowing and the voices of the animals were mumbled and faded.

I was afraid.

I woke up, gasping for breath, clinging to my chest as if the vines were still wrapped around my body.

I felt sick, but not the kind of sick where you could take cold medicine. Every time I thought of Rachel or my dream, my stomach tightened and would drop a few levels, as if I were on a fast-moving elevator toward the basement floor. My thoughts were driving me crazy; I couldn't sleep; I felt useless. I had to keep reminding myself who I was. I was nobody. I was out of her league. I thought being brave with Rachel was supposed to bring me opportunity and some sort of positive reward. I was trying to unlock a piece of my grid, but it didn't seem that I was very successful at it.

I took one last hopeless breath and felt my body relax as I exhaled. My room was growing dark; the sun was going down. I hadn't eaten all day and realized with a sudden pang that I was starving.

It seemed unusually quiet so I walked into the living room to check on my mother. She stood near the doorway, a brown paper bag of groceries in her grasp.

"Mom? What are you doing? Did you go to the store or something?"

She turned to look at me, her eyes lost and unfocused. I recognized that look instantly. Maybe she forgot her medication this morning. I usually supervised her while she took her pills, but today I had stayed in bed.

I watched her trying to focus on the thoughts that were forming. She had put makeup on her face, which wasn't like her. Her blush was extremely pink and bright; her eyes were dark with heavy eyeliner on her lower and upper lids. Her lipstick was a deep red and she had managed to get it all over her teeth.

"I'm waiting for my ride," she said.

"Where are you going, Mom?"

She turned her head to ignore me. I moved toward her and glanced inside the brown paper bag. Clothing and random snacks were tossed inside, along with a bottle of wine. I could tell she had been drinking because she wouldn't look at me, and she was agitated, not wanting to talk.

"Mom? Who's picking you up?" I was sure that no one was coming, but as soon as I asked the question, I heard a beep outside. My heart sank. I knew that she had called someone.

She opened the door.

"Mom, you can't leave just yet. I need to talk to you. It's important."

"It'll wait, Will. I'm leaving now."

"Where are you going, Mom? Do you even have money?"

My mother's eyes were determined as she continued on without answering my questions. I glanced at the kitchen table and noticed her pocketbook sitting there. She didn't even have her wallet. This had happened similarly when I was younger; I remember talking about it with my mother's therapist, who advised me to let her follow through with her behavior. *"Let her take herself to wherever she thinks she's going, and see what she does and what happens when she gets there."*

I didn't have time for that today. My father was picking me up and taking me out for pizza. It was a Saturday night tradition that we'd kept even throughout high school. I was usually home by 9:00, which meant I could still hang out with friends if I wanted to. It was hard to balance my parents at times. I was thankful for my father's low-maintenance attitude, because he was easy as far as time spent. We spoke occasionally on the phone during the week, but he didn't put a lot of pressure on me to spend time with him.

My mother, on the other hand—she wanted my time. If she didn't want me to go out, she put a guilt trip on me. It always started with her not feeling well or complaining that she felt dizzy and was worried she might fall or hurt herself. She had many ailments, according to her. We spent a lot of time at doctor's offices, and if she didn't like what one doctor said, she would go to another one. It wasn't often that she had an episode like this, and when it did happen, it was usually because of her lack of medication.

73

I followed her outside, watching her get into the cab. I had no idea she even knew how to call for a cab. The driver asked her where she was going. I waited, along with the driver, to hear what her response was. She looked confused and started to pick at the back of the driver's seat in front of her. The man waited patiently, and then asked her again. She looked at me.

"Will?" she asked.

"Mom, I don't know where you're going," I replied.

My mother exhaled deeply and folded her hands in her lap, annoyed that I didn't know what she was doing. I chuckled. "Mom, why don't you and I go inside and have another cup of tea?" I prayed she would agree to this. She hesitated, unmoving in the car, for what seemed like forever. Luckily, the man seemed to have an understanding that my mother was not well. The driver exited the car and opened my mother's door for her, and slowly she pulled herself out of the vehicle. I slipped the driver ten dollars and then held my mother's arm as we walked back into the house.

I always had to remind myself about the trauma from which my mother suffered. It helped me understand her more and to practice more patience. I loved my mother. I didn't want her to be afraid.

I called my father and told him I would be late to our dinner, but kept the call short. I didn't know how to explain this without causing concern. I needed to act normal, like everything was all right.

I washed my mother's face with a warm washcloth and gave her the medication along with a sleeping pill. She finally settled down, which was good, because I needed to see my father.

After I got ready, I stood outside on the stoop of our front porch, and when he promptly arrived we drove quietly down the street toward our favorite pizza place.

The restaurant was busy and the smells gave me energy. I was definitely hungry. My father ordered a beer and a pizza with everything on it, his favorite choice. I checked my phone a couple times, not sure what I was looking for but I checked anyway.

"How was the game last night?" my dad asked.

"Good. We won."

"Yeah? Seems like you have a good team this season?"

"We do, Dad."

"Have you given any more thought to what we talked about, regarding school next year?"

My dad wanted me to move away to college. He was willing to help me with the expenses and I had decent enough grades to get into a few of my choice schools, if I wanted to.

"It's not that easy, Dad."

My father sat back and cleared his throat, which meant I was about to get a lecture that I was in no mood for.

"You can't put off your life, Will, to take care of your mother."

I could feel anger start to swell up in my chest as he mentioned her. He had no idea what I did for her, or what I went through. I mean, she was my mother and I had no intention of abandoning her.

I adjusted my baseball cap.

"She's capable of figuring things out on her own," he went on. "She *could* manage without your help, you know. How will she learn anything if you keep assisting her?"

I took a sip of my soda; my head was starting to pound. "I don't want to talk about this, Dad. There's no reason why I can't commute back and forth to school and still live with her at home. It's not a big deal to me."

"You're missing out, Will. I don't think it should be your responsibility."

I shrugged. "Well whose responsibility is it then? I'm her only child. Are you kidding me? Just forget it, Dad, you don't understand."

My father did understand. He knew she was a depressed person; he knew that she was self-destructive and medicated. He couldn't possibly know how bad she was or about the episodes she had or the drinking. It wasn't his fault, really; I never told him. I never talked about it with anyone.

He could see that she was holding me back. I could see all the things he could, but I still couldn't bring myself to leave her. I wasn't willing to unlock that box for myself. What if I failed at being successful in life? Taking care of my mother gave me purpose. She needed me and that always made me feel good, to be needed. Besides, I was her son, and I was like her in a lot of ways.

I was afraid, too, of what life would look like if we both moved on and away from each other. Maybe she would be successful, but maybe I would fail and be alone. It scared me, to know the truth of it. It felt safer to stay with her and to have a purpose.

I threw my phone down on the table and walked to the bathroom. *Today can't get any worse*, I thought. *I just want my bed.*

77

I needed to punch something. Frustration flooded me but it felt kind of good to feel sorry for myself. Everybody sucked.

After I cooled down a bit, I returned to the table and watched my dad as he paid the bill. We walked away from the restaurant in silence and I sat in the car and stared out of the window as he drove me home. When my father pulled up to my house, he cleared his throat again.

I looked over at him, and waited.

"You know, Will, I only want what's best for you and your life. I want you to have the most opportunities that you can. Maybe you could consider that someday, you're going to have a wife and a family. What will you do then, for your mother? She needs to manage on her own or she'll never get past these problems of hers."

I stared at my dad. "I don't think you understand. I'm doing the best I can right now. I'm going to help my mom for as long as I can, and that's just how it is."

She had problems—they were real, and although some of them were self-imposed, others were not. She didn't know how to manage her life, and she didn't know how to open the boxes.

"When you feel the time is right, Will, I can help you. We will get the help she needs. Whether we bring people in or we send her out for care, there are options for her that would give you more freedom with your life."

I stood outside for a minute and leaned back into the car.

"I understand what you're saying, Dad. I'll cross those bridges when they come. Thanks for your concern, though. I'll see you next week."

My dad stared at me. "Yeah, okay. See you next week."

I slammed the door shut and walked up the sidewalk. The neighbors were fighting, which was no surprise. I looked along the fence line for the gypsy lady. I wanted to talk to her again. I wondered if she would ever come back.

In my bedroom, I collapsed onto my bed. A text from Alex popped up on my phone.

Hey, sorry about last night man. Everything okay?

I thought about not replying to him but he'd keep texting me if I didn't.

I'm fine. Just had dinner with my dad. EXHAUSTED.

His response came immediately. *Yikes, that bad?*

He wants me to go away to school.

Still? Maybe it's not such a bad idea.

Yeah, IDK. I put the phone down, not wanting to elaborate.

I know it's hard to consider, but I'm worried about you too. I don't want to see you sacrifice your future in order to keep your mom feeling safe and comforted. Maybe you can find one of those live-in ladies who can do things with your mom, like get her out of the house.

I scoffed as my fingers flew across the screen. *You sound just like my father.*

I understand where he's coming from. I know it's hard with your mother.

It was hard to keep everyone happy and not everyone knew the whole truth.

I'm tired, Alex. Thanks for texting.

No problem buddy. I know you need to make your own choices. Try to put yourself first sometimes, though. It's an important decision and I don't want to see you fuck up.

Yeah, okay, I'll think about it. Have a good night.

Good night Will."

My eyes were heavy and my heart still hurt but Alex made me feel better. That's what he was good at, and that's why I needed him.

He never made me feel alone.

Chapter
Eight

The next few weeks of school grew intense with studies. It was our final year and the last semester was upon us. High school graduation was looming; I had applied to the local state college and was accepted. My father seemed to understand this decision but kept the door open "just in case" I changed my mind. My mother seemed unimpressed that I had been accepted, which made the sacrifice to commute to school a little hard to swallow. I tried not to take it personally, but she was hurtful sometimes. It was clear she didn't care about what was best for me.

As the weeks passed, I seriously thought about what Alex and my father were trying to tell me. What would happen if I did leave her, if I opened that box and made different choices? It was hard to imagine seeing things in a different way. I wondered if that feeling would be gone, the guilt and dread, the depressed responsibility I seemed to carry around with me everywhere I went. I wondered if I could ever feel free of that...that *energy*. It really was energy—like being around Alex felt light and hopeful, whereas being around my mother felt dark sometimes, and repressed. It was hard to imagine life without that depressive energy, but I wondered.

Summer was coming and Alex and I had big plans for our last hurrah before college. I was going to work at the local movie theater. Alex worked at his father's construction company working on foundations. It was a hard job, labor intensive, but it suited him. He was tan and strong and the girls loved that about him.

I was looking forward to what was to come, even amidst my problems. I was hoping to spend time with Rachel.

Just a few final exams and I could breathe again. I'm not sure why studying mattered, because I had already made my college plans, but I didn't want to disappoint my teachers. They made it very clear to me what they expected. My teachers, for some reason, always pushed me harder to succeed. They believed in me, as a student and as a role model. I couldn't figure it out why they thought I was so special. So many other kids were smarter than me, better looking. But even still,

I appreciated their concern and extra efforts at trying to make something better out of me.

I was in deep thought as I made my way down the senior hallway toward my calculus class. I had an exam. I needed to concentrate but it was impossible; my responsibilities with my mother were on my mind.

Rachel sat next to me in class. "Are you okay?" she asked, turning to look at me.

I nodded and held her gaze and felt her concern for me, no longer stressed over the test, but lost in the degree of comfort and understanding from her.

"Okay class, you can begin now," Mr. Secundo said after passing out the tests.

I scanned the exam questions and focused on what needed to be done. The questions were familiar and I felt that I had a good handle on this test's topic. The class was filled with the sound of my classmates' pencils scratching and everyone had his or her head down in concentration.

Something caught my eye suddenly—Rachel. She had a pretty long-sleeved top on, lace and cotton. She kept glancing at her arms. Her sleeves were made of mostly lace…and as I looked, I could see that she had written on the insides of both her arms. Math formulas.

I looked away suddenly, as if I just discovered a rotten secret.

"William?" Mr. Secundo stated loud and abruptly.

It was too late. "Yes sir?" I replied.

"Rachel?"

Rachel looked up and stared blankly.

"Come with me, into the hallway."

Rachel stood from her chair and looked at me nervously. I shrugged and watched her as she wrapped her arms over each other and against her stomach. I followed her out into the hallway.

Mr. Secundo glared at me, disappointment in his expression.

"William, this seems so out of character for you. I saw you looking at Rachel's paper."

Rachel looked over at me, her blue eyes rounded in fear. She looked so scared and uncertain, but beautifully vulnerable.

"Mr. Secundo, I promise you I was not looking at Rachel's paper. I was distracted, that's all, and honestly, I studied all night and I'm pretty confident I can pass this exam easily."

Mr. Secundo looked over at Rachel. "I apologize, Rachel. I just wanted you to be aware that he was looking at your work."

Rachel's face was bright red and when she began to speak, her voice wavered, as if she might cry. "I'm sure he didn't mean to, Mr. Secundo. William has always been an honest student."

I thought about telling the truth about her and the inside of her arms, but only for a split second. I couldn't imagine embarrassing her like that. Besides, she looked so desperate.

Mr. Secundo took one last look at me. "Take your test and chair out into the hallway, William. You can finish the exam out here."

I rolled my eyes. *This day can't possibly get any worse.*

I took my pencil and paper and chair out of the classroom and into the hallway like a little kid.

I took a deep breath and began to fill in my answers. I wasn't sure if any of this was worth it. Rachel was worth it, I guess. Being banished to the hallway to take my test wasn't such a bad thing. *Better me than her*, I thought, realizing that if Mr. Secundo had seen the answers written on her arms, she would likely be suspended.

I wrote my answers down.

I was doing this for Rachel.

Chapter

Nine

The events of the next day came as a surprise to me. I was content in dragging myself to school, still stressed over yesterday's debacle. Alex had picked me up in front of my house, like usual. When he couldn't, I took the bus. My mother was still sleeping when I left; my first class was at 7:35 AM.

Alex parked in the senior parking lot and we began to walk toward the building.

A few classmates joined us, leading us into the school's main entrance. It was one of those mornings where the clouds were heavy and the sun hadn't quite made its appearance yet. The pavement was damp and the air was thick with moisture. The weather made me want to stay in bed all day and hide underneath my covers just a little longer.

I heard my name being called. "Will! Will, wait up!"

It was Rachel. I turned around and faced her as she caught up to me; her step was quick and she was out of breath. She handed me a Starbucks coffee. I took the drink, grateful for the warmth it offered and for the aroma of hazelnut.

"Hey, I wanted to thank you for yesterday…for not telling Mr. Secundo the truth about me," she began. I saw the shame settle across her face. "I don't want you to think I'm a bad person. I have never cheated before." Rachel's hand was shaking as her emotions began to fill the corners of her eyes. I could hear her words, but what surprised me was her genuine appreciation and the thoughtful coffee. All I could do was stare at her blankly.

She shook her head in embarrassment. "I was worried about the final—I couldn't afford to fail—and I know it was awful and stupid of me, but I couldn't risk it. My stepfather would have killed me. I hope you understand." She paused. "I've promised myself to never do this again. "

I nodded with an open mouth, hoping something smart and consoling would come out of it. Alex appeared behind me and placed his hand on my shoulder and shook me.

"Hey Rachel, what's going on?" I knew he was silently encouraging me as he squeezed my shoulder. "William is thankful for the coffee," he added. "He's quite the hero, isn't he?"

Rachel smiled back at Alex—it was hard not to; he carried that joy with him wherever he went.

Rachel looked at me and I finally managed to smile just before she reached up and kissed me on my cheek. She whispered, "I owe you one," then turned and walked energetically into the high school.

Alex looked at me sideways and nodded in approval. "Well, would you look at that?" he stated sarcastically.

"I did her a favor, that's all," I replied.

But then I smiled. I guess yesterday wasn't as bad as I thought. I suddenly felt hope again—I was excited about something. Rachel made me feel good, like sitting at night on my porch and watching the stars fill the sky, or listening to the crickets in the middle of a warm summer evening. She felt lovely.

I had Alex. Alex fit me like a glove, and from the minute we first met we were best friends. It felt like that with Rachel too. We were connected; our energy was the same in the way that we just fit somehow, and I knew we fit even though we hadn't progressed that far in our friendship.

The box was finally opening; things were starting to happen because of the few brave choices that I made. Maybe the gypsy was actually onto something. Maybe she was right.

Just a simple gesture of a coffee but I knew in that moment: I was going to have a good day.

Chapter

Ten

My body was turning pink as the scalding water rained down on me from our outdated showerhead. I felt calm for the moment...until I stepped out of the shower and heard the insistent banging on the door. My mother was racing around the house from one room to another, looking out windows and trying to articulate to me what was going on. I was barely dry but I could see the flash of lights from the front yard, and when I looked out, multiple police cruisers blocked our driveway *and* the neighbor's driveway for what sure was to be another domestic incident.

The banging was getting more frantic so I walked toward the back of the house to see what was the matter. Peeking out of the small window next to the backyard door, I saw my neighbor John standing there, a bag in his hand. I opened the back door and tried to hold my temper.

"More trouble, John?" I asked dryly. He was such a loser, a real lowlife. His teeth were in bad shape and he rarely had a haircut. His jeans were ragged and too big for his scrawny posture. He was an alcoholic. He sat around all day drinking, contributing nothing to his family. And now he was standing on my back porch.

"You need to take this for me, man." John shoved a brown lunch bag full of *something* in my hand.

"What is it?" I asked but before he could answer, he jumped down off my porch and ran into another neighbor's yard. I could hear the police scanner in the distance and a child's cry through my neighbor's windows.

I secured my back door and locked it. Before my mother could see, I walked into my bedroom and closed my door.

I stared at the bag. It felt heavy and full and I could smell its contents, the aroma filling my room. It was weed. Fresh grown, fresh cut, pure and wonderful weed.

I opened the bag to confirm what I already knew and was impressed with the amount that was magically given to me. "Yes, yes, yes!" I sang, doing a happy dance, my heart still racing from the dramatic exchange just a few seconds before.

I threw my towel up over my closet door and got dressed. I took the bag of weed and placed it in another plastic bag to hide the odor and then wrapped a towel around it, shoving it neatly into my backpack. Alex would be at my house shortly and this couldn't have come at a better time. We were heading to an end-of-school-year party at Leslie's house. Her parents were out of town and she lived up on Parker Lane, a well-to-do area just north of here. Her house was big and gorgeous, with an in-ground pool, a rec room with a pool table, foosball, and beer pong. It was like being on vacation at her house.

"William!" my mother yelled. "Alex is here."

I walked out into the kitchen with my backpack, my cheeks hurting slightly from the smile on my face. Alex was in my living room, talking with my mother. I couldn't help but feel happy. It was obvious that tonight, I was going to be someone important at this party.

"Hey Alex!" I said brightly. "You hungry?" I threw him a can of Coca Cola.

"No thanks. I was just telling your mom here"—Alex had his arm wrapped around my mother, shining his charm down upon her—"that if she wanted me to, I could go next door to investigate what's happening, to make sure she's nice and safe before we leave tonight."

My mother smiled up at Alex with her bright eyes. Those words were like magic to her; she loved the attention.

"Oh Alex." She laughed innocently. "I'll be just fine." My mother looked up at him with a little mischief in her expression. "Besides, I think the neighbors might be in a little bit of trouble."

"You don't say?" Alex responded dramatically. "Come on Will, let's take a quick look for your mom. I know she's dying to find out the truth."

The chemistry between Alex and my mom was instantaneous from the first day they met each other. My mother loved Alex just as much as I did and he seemed to understand her needs intuitively. I left my backpack on the living room couch and followed Alex down the stoop of our front porch until we reached the first patrol car, which blocked my driveway.

Alex hunched down to speak to the officer sitting in the car. "Good evening sir!"

The officer glanced up at us, then opened the door and stepped out of his vehicle. "Hello boys. What can I do for you?"

"Well, my friend and his mother live in this house…"

I nodded in acknowledgement as the officer looked at me. "Yes, I wanted to make sure that everything was okay, Officer. My mother is concerned for her safety."

The officer folded his arms across his body. "What is your mother's name?" He reached out his hand to shake mine.

"Linda," I replied.

"Tell your mother everything is fine. Your neighbors have a series of outstanding warrants that need to be addressed, but we have things under control. Thank you for your concern, but there is no real need to worry."

Alex replied, "These guys are real interesting folks, huh Officer?"

The officer smiled but remained professional as he re-entered his police cruiser. "Have a nice night, boys," he said.

Alex and I returned to my mother, who was staring out of the window, watching us intently.

Alex was first through the door. "Nothing to worry about, Mrs. D. Just some outstanding warrants. You're perfectly safe. The officer promised to watch over you while we are gone."

My mother threw her arms around Alex in a strong, motherly hug. "Thank you, Alex. I feel much better now."

Alex looked down into her face. "I know you do." He walked her over to the couch and sat her down. Alex knew the routine with my mother. He also knew that if I felt she was safe tonight, I'd have a better time at the party.

What he didn't know, though, was what I had in my *backpack*.

"Will, I'm sure your mom wants her cup of tea now."

"Oh yes Will, that would be lovely."

Alex turned on the TV and chatted mindlessly with my mother as I got her things ready. I placed her tea on the side table near the couch and reached down to kiss her goodbye. "You okay, Mom?" I asked.

"I'm fine, honey."

Alex also kissed my mother goodbye. "Goodnight, Mrs. D."

"Not too late Will," she responded with a smile.

"Okay, love you, Mom."

I grabbed my backpack and shut and locked the door behind me.

"Where did you park?" I asked Alex as we walked past the police cars.

"I had to park a ways because the police blocked the road."

When we were far enough away from the cops, I patted Alex roughly on the back, my enthusiasm barely under control. He looked over at me, his face revealing his confusion over the sudden excitement in my step and in my eyes.

"You are *not* going to believe this…"

Chapter
Eleven

Alex insisted that I sell some of the weed and pocket a little money for my trouble. He said he would handle it, so I gave him half the bag and let him do his thing. The other half I wanted to share. I wanted to be like Santa Claus, walking into a room with a whole bunch of toys for small children. I wanted everyone to like me, to enjoy what I had to offer them, to think I was the greatest. Walking in to that party, I felt a wave of power and confidence flow over me.

It wasn't long before word got out. I stationed myself in the kitchen among the countertops layered with bags of chips and dips and miscellaneous desserts. The kitchen was massive, at least bigger than any kitchen I'd ever been in. I leaned against the counter and emptied the weed on the granite. I rolled several joints. The first few were ugly; my fingertips stuck to the paper and tiny bits of weed stuck to my lips.

98

Big Joe watched with amusement until he finally pushed me out of the way and did the job for himself. "Boyyyy, you have no idea what you're doing. Get the hell out of here before I kick your ass."

I stepped out of the way and let him do what he did best. It didn't look complicated, but he definitely had a certain skill set that I lacked and I was impressed with his abilities. I made a conscious decision that I would practice more and get better at it…in the privacy of my own bedroom, away from the eyes of Big Joe and the others.

"I'll be right back, you want a beer?"

"Yeah, that's cool," he said, the cigarette paper and folded green bud in between his fingers.

I walked through the house and filled two red cups with cold beer from the keg. Leslie stood across the room and waved. She seemed happy to see me. I lifted the cups over my head and moved through the living room space, which had been transformed into a dance floor. Christmas lights hung from the tall ceiling and the couches had been pushed to the sides of the wall. My buddy Jake was manning the radio system. Music blasted. I said hey to everyone I passed, my head held high and proud. I couldn't believe my luck. I wondered briefly if Rachel would be at the party and I secretly held hope that we could spend time together.

"Here you go, Big Joe!" I placed the cup full of beer on the counter next to about fifteen rolled joints. "Holy shit," I stated, amazed at his skill and speed.

"Not bad huh?" Big Joe had deep dimples when he smiled and his teeth were perfectly straight. His face was round and friendly and he smelled clean, like fresh out of a shower clean. He was a big boy, about 270 pounds and six feet tall. The girls loved him because he was funny.

Alex walked into the kitchen with a bottle of whiskey in one hand and a wad of cash in the other. He slapped the cash in my hand and I started to count it.

"FIVE HUNDRED DOLLARS!" I exclaimed.

"Shhh... Jeez, Will. Take it easy."

This kind of money could change my life. My mother's disability check only went so far and some of her medications cost a lot of money. I needed things too, like new sneakers, and I would like to buy a new car at some point.

I eyed Alex as he boosted himself on the granite counter, looking over Big Joe's handiwork. *I wonder if Alex would help me buy more weed.* "You gonna light one of those bad boys, Joe, or what?" Alex asked.

Big Joe turned around with a joint hanging out of his mouth. "You got a light?"

Alex reached deep into his pocket and produced a black lighter.

Big Joe took a few solid hits of the joint, then handed it over to Alex. Alex held it in his fingers for a few seconds and inspected it. He put the cigarette to his lips and sucked hard as the red cherry lit up the end.

"It's not bad," he ground out, coughing through tight lips. He passed the joint to me and I took a hit, waiting a few seconds before exhaling. I had never been a big pot smoker, but I occasionally smoked at parties or with Alex.

More friends had joined the circle, so Big Joe lit another joint and began passing it around the kitchen in the opposite direction. "This is from Will, you guys," he said. The others looked at me appreciatively, telling me thanks.

I felt a small arm wrap around my waist; when I looked down, I was surprised to see that it was Rachel. She looked up at me and smiled, squeezing my side. I glanced over at Alex who nodded at me, a cheesy grin on his face.

"Hey Will." Rachel slurred her words a little. She had been drinking, that was obvious. I took another hit then passed the joint to her. She smiled and inhaled the smoke, then passed it to her girlfriend who stood beside her. "I was hoping to run into you tonight."

My head swooned briefly and my body relaxed as I drank down my beer. My insides warmed as I felt Rachel's arm wrapped around me. It felt right in so many ways. Rachel was much shorter than me and although I tried not to look, I could see her cleavage perfectly clear down to her white lace bra. She looked plump and soft and I tried not to stare.

Leslie appeared with a few other girls.

"Hey guys, did you hear about what happened over at West Elm High School last week?"

I looked at Leslie, curious.

"It was really weird—some of the students had been complaining that chairs and tables were being moved around, randomly, in one of their classrooms. They thought maybe the custodian was messing with them, stacking the chairs on top of each other awkwardly, and sometimes the tables were flipped upside down. This went on for weeks, until finally someone installed a hidden camera. When they were able to view the footage, it was obvious that there was some metaphysical activity going on."

Leslie had the attention of everyone in the kitchen.

"You know, metaphysical, like ghost and spirits and all things supernatural, the spirit world."

"I don't know if I believe in all that shit," Big Joe stated.

Alex buried his head into Leslie's neck and yelled, "Boo!" Leslie's shoulders cringed as she rolled her eyes.

"Anyway," she continued, "on the footage of the tape you can see someone standing behind a door, and the image of a face through the window."

"What did the principal do about it? That's super creepy. I don't think I would want to be in that classroom," Rachel commented.

Alex looked at me. "Tell them about the gypsy you met."

I raised my eyes and took a breath. The gypsy still haunted me, although I took her words about the boxes and staying on the right path seriously. The parts of her warning me about the danger I was in, I tried to forget. I didn't want to give it any energy.

"I like to think there's something more out there, that exists outside of us," I shared as I looked down at Rachel. She smiled up at me, uninterested in the conversation of our peers that continued as we focused our stare on one another.

"What gypsy?" she asked.

"I met this woman recently. She talked about magic and how we all have grids and boxes to unlock and pathways to follow, and how positive decisions open more boxes and lead to more positive life experiences."

"That sounds nice," Rachel stated.

"Tell them what else," Alex said.

"She warned me about my path. She said I was in danger and to watch the decisions that I made."

It hadn't dawned on me, but I started to think about the weed Alex sold and the money. This had to be a good decision for me. My mother and I needed money, and bringing the weed was making me popular with my classmates. I was starting to belong somewhere—*finally*. Like I was finally being useful to people, to my friends. It was a win-win. What harm could it cause?

"I don't think your life is in danger. I think you make really good decisions," Rachel added.

"Yeah but maybe we're all in danger because the school is haunted." Alex grabbed his throat with his hands and pretended to choke himself. "Maybe we should all skip class on Monday." He laughed.

I ignored him. "I've been trying to follow her advice, or at least be more aware of my own fears and the choices that I make. I've been trying to be more brave, and it seems to have had a definite positive effect on some people."

My insides fired up and I looked at Rachel, whose genuine smile filled me. I took this still moment to bend down and kiss her softly. She didn't hesitate and reached up to meet me halfway, squeezing me tightly around my back.

I took another hit of the joint that made its way around and Rachel started to pull on me. "It's a good story, Leslie," I said as I winked at her, following Rachel out of the room.

"Come on, Will. Let's dance." Rachel giggled and stumbled as she walked backward. I followed her, unsure of my dance moves but feeling confident in my newfound popularity among my friends. We bumped into a few people before we were able to find our space, a few hands clapping me on the back alongside appreciative comments. I could feel the room spin and slowed the dance down to a subtle rock with Rachel in my arms.

We stayed like this for several songs, my head cloudy from the marijuana, my thoughts filled with Rachel.

"Do you want to go somewhere?" she whispered.

I nodded, following her back into the kitchen, we stole another joint off the counter, snatched a few bottles of beer, then escaped outside into the backyard.

"Come on Will, I know a little place where we could be alone."

I followed her without question to the small tool shed at the back of the property. We passed several other students as we walked along the pool area and I welcomed the high fives and the occasional "There's the guy!" comments. The weed I brought to the party was a big hit. I was full of an energy I had never quite experienced before. It felt amazing.

Rachel pushed open the side door of the shed, which was partially blocked by rakes and random bags of potting soil. I helped her clear a small space and set out a couple of broken-down lawn chairs. Delicately I sat. The tangled bottom of one chair fell apart; I could see my butt hanging down between the pieces of vinyl and the dusty dirt floor beneath it.

"Oh my god, Will," Rachel gasped, laughing, "I don't think that chair is going to make it."

She was right. "This isn't looking good for me." I smirked as I stood up carefully. I folded the chair and threw it behind the lawn mower toward the back of the shed. "Your chair looks perfect though, doesn't it?"

I reached for Rachel's hand and dragged her out of the seat as I sat in it. Pulling her back down on my lap, we settled in comfortably, with her in my arms.

It was easy between us. It felt comfortable, the way she had her fingers in my hair and her sigh when she leaned in close. We stayed like this, staring at the unopened bottles of beer and the unsmoken joint on the windowsill.

"Will?"

"Yeah," I answered.

"Do you worry about college?" Rachel turned to look at me. "Do you worry when all this is over—high school, I mean—if you're making the right decisions?"

Her eyes were uncertain and I started to understand why she may have wanted to cheat on her exams.

"I worry about other things, Rachel. I worry about my mother and taking care of her. My education will come and I hope that I make the right decisions, but I don't really have many choices in the matter. I need to care for my mother."

Rachel raised her chin. "What's wrong with your mother?"

"She has a hard time taking care of things, herself mainly, so I try to be available. I try to do what I can for

107

her. She's taking medication for her problems, but it could still be challenging and hard at times." I reached up to grab the two beers with her still in my arms.

"Oh my god, you're going to drop me!" She laughed.

I smiled mischievously and opened her bottle for her. We drank them and fell deeper into each other on the chair.

"Is that why you're not going away to college?" she asked.

My stomach sank in the way she felt disappointment for me, as if going away to college were the only answer. I wondered if I had made the right choice. It wasn't a hard decision, but it felt like a lonely one. No one seemed to support it. No one seemed to understand.

I placed the back of my hand on her cheek and brushed her skin softly. "Your face is so soft," I said, "and your eyes sparkle with this color blue I can only imagine exists just to drive boys like me crazy."

Rachel's round cheeks grew warm and red as the corners of her mouth flirted with a smile. "You say the nicest things to me; it's almost hard to believe that they're true." I thought about Andrew and how rude he was to her, how he probably never had anything nice to say. I wondered if she still cared for him.

"Rachel, you're the nicest girl in the entire school. I could count how many times you've said hello to me—fifteen in total this year." I paused and squeezed her gently around her waist. "Hello Will!" My voice was sharp but sweet as I imitated her perfectly. She leaned her head onto my shoulder and I could feel her body shake as she laughed.

"You're just teasing me," she commented.

"Wait, I have one question for you though. I don't understand why you always have all those books in your arms, and the binders? You take everything you own to every class you have. It's like you're a walking library or something."

She was always one bump away from tossing everything she carried onto the floor of our high school hallway. I wanted to be there when it happened. I wanted to help her clean the mess she had made and make her laugh at herself.

The corner of Rachel's eyes watered as she adjusted herself in my lap, her words heavy with a pain that was real. "I'm afraid that if I'm not perfect, or if I forget something, then I'll fail and that I'll disappoint my teachers." When she looked up at me, she was breathtakingly vulnerable. I wanted to make it better for her. "I don't want to disappoint anyone." She lowered her eyes.

I thought of ways I could try to ease Rachel's fears about college and grades and the pressures of school. I tried to give her the strength that I wasn't even sure I felt, but in that moment, I did.

"I have a hard time with my stepfather," she said. "He has the highest expectations of me and when I don't meet those expectations, he treats me as if I were this horrible person." Rachel shock her head. "I don't understand it. I try to please him and he's never pleased."

It was hard not to badmouth her stepfather, because I knew he was a jerk, but I knew that wouldn't be helpful. "Soon, you'll be moving on and away from your parents, Rachel. His problems with you won't be your problems anymore. You'll be free from it."

But I would never feel free, I realized. I was trapped—just like she was—except she was going to escape, and I was not. I would never take my own advice. I made my mother's problems my own and I couldn't seem to find a way around that.

Her fingers were delicate as she placed her hand underneath my shirt. I continued to talk, recognizing that things were growing more intimate between us. I wasn't sure what to do; I had never been with a girl before and all the confidence and power I had felt earlier was suddenly fleeing my body, replaced by insecurity and an awful voice inside my head, telling me I would do this all wrong.

Rachel kissed my face and she moved closer to me on the chair, straddling her legs over the sides so that her chest faced mine. She began to unbutton her shirt and I could see her breasts in the shadows of the night, her white lace bra the only lightness in the darkened room. I had imagined this scenario many times before, and now it was happening. *Today is awesome.*

"Rachel, are you sure about this? I want you to be sure. We don't need to do this."

"Please Will, I don't want to go to college a virgin. I'm afraid of what people will think of me." She laughed. "Besides, I really like you."

"But here, in this shed? Are you sure we should do this?"

"Yes," she said, unbuttoning my pants. She stood to take off her underwear. I felt like I was dreaming, my eyes never leaving hers, not even for a second. I helped her slide back onto my lap thinking I had died and gone to Heaven. My emotions were overflowing and I could

111

not in my lifetime have imagined how wonderful a naked woman's body would feel against my skin.

***

When we finished, Rachel appeared to be relieved, but she was quick to get dressed and was eager to return to the party before anyone began to search for us.

I got dressed, then kissed and thanked her. She thanked me, too, as if we just handed each other another hazelnut coffee latte from Starbucks. I felt panicked on the inside, not wanting this to get weird between us. Before she hurried out of the shed, I took her hand in my hand.

"Rachel! We need to do something funny. Remember the story Leslie told in the kitchen?"

Rachel's face seemed to relax. "Yes, I do."

"Let's set up the shed right now, putting items on top of each other like the high school classroom in Leslie's story."

Rachel held her stomach and covered her mouth. "Oh my god Will, she'll freak out!"

"I know, let's do it and then I can give you a ride home."

Rachel and I worked together, moving things around quickly in the shed. We were proud of our practical joke and only hoped Leslie would notice come morning. Things felt normal between us again. I felt relieved for the moment, but as our eyes met, we shared a knowing glance: Something had permanently changed between us.

I understood things were never going to be the same.

Chapter
Twelve

Rachel said she felt nauseous as I pulled up to her house around 12:30 AM. The car ride seemed endless and I could tell Rachel struggled to keep her focus on the dashboard. I hoped that she wouldn't get sick.

I helped her up the driveway, the keys to the front door slipping out of her hand as she managed to move up the front steps toward her house, holding on to the railing to steady herself. I bent over to grab them, falling back onto the grass of her perfectly manicured front lawn. I laid there, willing myself to get up, knowing that Rachel needed me and not wanting to wake her mother and stepfather, but it was too late.

"Rachel?" His voice was deep, dripping with annoyance.

Rachel stood tall and at full attention as she faced him, avoiding making direct eye contact. "Yes sir," she stated softly.

"What time is it?" Rachel's stepfather opened the front door and took a few steps toward her as she sucked in her breath, concealing the smell of beer, which was sure to be noticeable.

"It's just after midnight."

He stared at her, his face stone cold and lacking emotion. Her stepfather had raised her and she always seemed grateful for the life he had given her and her mother, but it was obvious he showed no feeling toward her. He did what was right; he made sure they had a home, food to eat, a safe place to live. He held high expectations for her and assumed that she would do the right things too—study hard, clean the house, and be respectful. Emotionally, he lacked zero empathy for her. He had been hard on her for her entire life, and I wasn't sure she knew what it was to feel true affection or love from a man.

Rachel stood her ground as I heard him inhale deeply then exhale, a sense of frustration building inside of him.

"You're late."

I stood up finally and took my place next to Rachel. "I'm very sorry, sir. This is my fault. I had promised to bring her home earlier, but I had car trouble and we needed to stop at the gas station." I placed my hand on Rachel's back, hoping he would redirect his irritation at me, because I could handle it.

Rachel's stepfather was a military man, a twenty-year retired general. Perhaps this was why he never smiled, made jokes, or showed joy. Rachel once conveyed to me that as a child she would sit up at night and say her prayers with her mother. She would pray that her stepfather would go to work and never come back. There were periods in her childhood where he would be gone for months at a time—and these were the happiest moments of her life. Her mother would dote on her, show love openly by kissing her face, expressing how beautiful and special she was. She shared memories of walks around the pond catching frogs and eating ice cream at 10:00 at night, and then they would sleep together in the same bed, talk and giggle like two little girls. Rachel said she would wrap her arms around her mother and sleep peacefully, her heart full. She loved her mother; she never understood why she'd married such a hardened man.

Rachel's stepfather seemed unmoved by my admittance of guilt, but appeared to concede anyway. "We'll talk about this more in the morning. Go to bed now."

"Yes, I will. I'm so sorry, sir."

He turned abruptly and walked back into the house.

Rachel closed her eyes and placed her hands over her heart. I thought she might hyperventilate. Her stepfather scared her.

"I'm so sorry Will, I didn't mean for this to happen."

"You better go inside now. I don't want to upset him any further."

Rachel nodded and kissed me lightly on the cheek. She said goodnight and walked into her house, locking the door behind her.

I got into my car to drive back home. I had several missed calls from Alex. I dialed his number.

"Hey, don't ask me any questions about Rachel. I'm not willing to talk about it."

"It's not about that. It's my parents. Can you come here?"

Alex was upset and I knew instinctively that the shit must be hitting the fan.

"I'll be right over, buddy. I'm on my way."

I hung up the phone, knowing that I had a long night ahead of me. I drove over to Alex's, worried about what to expect. Several cars were in the driveway and I immediately recognized his mom's sister's car. I parked and walked up the long sidewalk toward the front door. Alex opened it before I could knock; I could tell he was still buzzed from Leslie's party.

"This is bullshit," he spewed. "It's like an intervention on my mom. They have her trapped in a room, talking to her as if she was a child, and everyone is against her. My aunt is there, my father *and* Angie's husband."

Alex's words were panicked, as if they were going to hurt his mother in some way.

"Okay, okay, calm down. What do you mean she's trapped?"

"They won't let her out, and they won't let me in. I don't know, but she's alone and they're all taking turns yelling at her, telling her she doesn't know what she's doing and that she's making a huge mistake."

Alex stepped back inside the hallway and I followed him. "Where's Angie?" I asked.

"I tried to call her, but she didn't answer. I left her a message. I don't think she knows what's going on." We walked around the kitchen and moved through the living room toward the back of the house where Alex's father's office was. Inside, I could hear the voices talking over each other. Occasionally Alex's dad would yell, unable to control his anger.

118

Oh God, this can't be good.

Alex stood outside the door and leaned his forehead on it.

"What do you want to do, Alex?"

"I want her out of there. They all know now that she loves Angie, and they need to process what's happening. They're not going to figure this out tonight and I'm not going to sit back and watch them abuse my mother. I know it's not an easy situation, and maybe I've had a little more time to digest things, but I was never cruel to my mother. She doesn't deserve this."

I took a deep breath. I wasn't sure what to do, but Alex and his mom needed my support. I pushed Alex aside from the door. Maybe I could be a voice of reason and understanding. Maybe I could help them. I knocked on the door, loudly.

"Mr. Davanport? It's William. I need to talk to you, sir. I need you to open this door." I paused and waited while the voices on the other side remained quiet. "Hello? Do you hear me? We would like to come in please."

Alex and I looked at each other and waited. I could hear footsteps rapidly approach and the lock clicked open, the energy on the other side of the door thick with drama and emotion. We stood staring into the

119

room while the occupants stared back. Alex's mother sat on a sofa, her eyes red and swollen, her body posture defeated and unsure.

"Mom!" Alex moved through the room toward her. He sat and took her hand while she hugged him.

She placed her hand on his face. "I'm okay Alex. I don't want you to worry about this. We're just talking."

I watched her eyes. She wasn't convincing, not for a second. Alex's dad walked behind his desk and sat down with an open bottle of whisky. He poured himself a shot. I felt bad for him, but not as bad as I felt for his mother.

"Did you kids know? Did you know all about this, that your mother is a *dyke*?" Alex's aunt was full of accusation. Her words startled me, because they were so offensive. I hadn't heard that word in a long time, and in fact, I didn't know people still used it. She seemed very ignorant, the way she talked and the aggression she held for her sister.

Alex was red in the face. "Why are you here?" he asked her. "This situation has nothing to do with you. It's between my mother and my father."

"Your father has asked me to be here," she said, her hands landing on her hips. "I'm here for my sister's sake. This *relationship* is not going to happen—not to your family and not to ours. It's an embarrassment, and you should be very ashamed of your mother."

Alex stood and started to pace the room. I recognized that energy before; he was trying to stay respectful to his aunt, but it was hard for him.

"How do you feel, Alex? Do you think this is *normal?* What about your friends? Aren't you embarrassed for what they might think of you?"

Alex paused abruptly in front of his aunt. "I have thought about this over and over again and yes, it does make me feel uncomfortable. I don't want to have to explain it to my friends and I wish that my parents could stay married and be happy." Alex looked shyly at his mother. "But I love my mother. I have a great deal of respect for her and I know that this is hard for her too."

Alex's mother looked lovingly at him.

"This takes time getting used to—it doesn't happen overnight—and I feel like everything will be fine, eventually. Like…people will get over this and my mother will be happy and that's what matters the most to me."

I stood back against the door to the bathroom, away from the middle of the office, watching the tangled mess unfold. It was interesting how Alex's mom's ability to open one box now challenged her own family, forcing them to open their own boxes. Some were choosing to stay positive, while others were closed-minded, following the path of negativity. Her sister was already labeling her. Labels were so stupid and ignorant—I learned this with my mother. People called her *crazy,* as if that were some sort of medical diagnosis. My mother didn't need to be labeled, and neither did Alex's mother. A word didn't determine who or what they were.

Alex approached his father, anger laced in his voice. "This doesn't need to be this way. You're handling this all wrong. I know you feel hurt right now, but Mom deserves your respect and understanding. She's always been good to you. I know this. I've lived this."

Alex's father looked disappointed as he took a sip of his drink, without responding.

Alex's mom finally stood and smoothed her dress. "Alex, honey, come here and stand by me." Alex walked toward his mother and she took his hand. She looked him in his eyes and smiled deeply. "Thank you Alex. Thank you for your support. I'm so very proud of you."

My best friend was hurting, but he was ready and willing to defend his mother. The way his eyes looked— fierce and determined.

"I know that you all think this is a mistake. I know that you can't possibly understand this, because you've never experienced this for yourselves. This isn't your path to walk, but it is mine and I am very confident that I am making the right decisions for myself. I love Angie and I'm going to be with her. You don't have to agree with it. I'm not asking you to, but I hope that eventually, you will come around and support me. We are a family and I love all of you."

As she was speaking, Angie appeared in the doorway, her face full of concern and love. She smiled and walked confidently into the room. Her look was challenging, as though she welcomed anyone to stand up to her, to speak their mind. I glanced around the room; not one person would meet her challenge. Not one person but Alex's mother met her stare. Her strength was tangible.

Alex's mother walked toward Angie and held onto her hand tightly.

"Are you okay?" Angie asked.

"Yes, I'm fine."

"Are you ready?"

"Yes," she replied with a bright smile on her face.

They turned and walked out of the office together.

***

123

Alex followed them outside and his mother reassured him that she was okay.

"We've got a small place to stay for now. I think it's best we let your father absorb this, let it settle in. I'll be back tomorrow to get more things and we can talk then."

"Okay, Mom. I love you."

"I love you too, Alex."

And that was it. It was over. Everything was out in the open.

Chapter

Thirteen

I hadn't seen Rachel or Alex in school all day. I was worried about them both; their families seemed upside down and I was starting to feel a sense of stability in my own. I wanted to talk with Rachel, hoping she wasn't avoiding me, but someone had mentioned that she might have gone home early. At 7:00 I planned to call her, and I wanted to have a plan of action. Maybe make a list of conversation topics, or questions that I could ask her in case the conversation went silent. This would be the first time we spoke on the phone, so I wanted it to go well.

Alex needed time, I understood. He was in a tough situation, but I was proud of the support he showed for his mother. He was staying positive, which always suited him best; he carried that light with him.

"William?"

I looked up from my chair. My mother was standing in the kitchen, her winter coat draped around her shoulders.

"What are you doing, Mom? It's eighty degrees outside."

"I'm cold," she said flatly.

I took the coat from her and returned it to the hallway closet. She looked at me as if I just took a bag of Halloween candy away from her.

"Will, when do you think the neighbor will be back?"

"I don't know, Mom, hopefully never."

We were having the same conversation every day, about the neighbor and his arrest.

"What will happen though, if he does? We should move."

"We can't afford to move, Mom. It's no big deal. The neighbor can't hurt us."

I watched my mother walk over to the window. "Will? Do you think the neighbor knows things about me?"

I was confused by her question. Although my mother often confused me, I was curious. "What things, Mom?"

My mother stared off.

126

"Mom?"

Silence.

My neighbor was arrested for violating a child support order and assaulting an officer. It wasn't like he murdered someone, but my mother couldn't understand that. I wondered perhaps he'd come looking for his weed if he returned, but Carol reassured me that he was gone forever. She said the court sentenced him to over ten years in prison. He was never coming back.

I had other thoughts on my mind, anyway. I still had five hundred dollars in my pocket. It would be cool to turn it into one thousand dollars. I had a call into a guy that Alex knew, a dealer. I wanted to meet him. I wanted to make more money and I wanted to make more friends.

"Ma?"

My mother was still at the window.

"You want some tea, Mom?"

She looked over at me. I could tell by her eyes that it was time to wind her down.

I walked over to her and put my arm around her shoulder. "I love you, Mom."

She nodded silently.

I sat her in her spot on the couch and went into the kitchen. When I made the tea I dissolved a sleeping agent in it, which the doctor had given her but she never used. I was sorry to do it, but it made my life easier sometimes and she rested through the night without waking.

After putting several cookies on a plate, I walked over to her and placed the snack on the TV tray next to the couch. I handed her the cup of tea.

"Thank you William," she said quietly.

I kissed her on her forehead and walked out of the living room and into my bedroom. It was 7:00 on the dot.

I picked up my phone and dialed Rachel's phone number.

I was nervous but I wanted to get it over with. I felt awkwardness about what had happened between us, and we needed to talk about it.

The phone rang.

"Hello," she answered.

"Hey Rach, it's me. Will."

There was a pause. "Hey Will."

"I hope you're not busy."

"No, it's okay. It's fine."

"I didn't see you in school today."

There was another pause on the other end of the line. "I know, I wasn't feeling well. I decided to leave early."

"So, about the other night. Are you okay? I was hoping we could talk about what happened."

I could hear her breathing on the phone. Her voice seemed still, a slight tinge of irritation.

"Everyone knows," she stated matter-of-factly.

I was shocked by her statement. I hadn't told anyone; even though Alex and Big Joe tried to pry it out of me, I hadn't given them any details. I mean, people knew that we disappeared together. People saw us go into the shed, but...

"I'm sorry that people know," I said. "I didn't tell anyone. It's just rumors Rachel; no one knows what really happened."

"It was a big mistake Will...I didn't mean it. It's just, you were so nice to me, and the beer, and..."

"It's okay, Rachel," I said, as realization settled over me. "It's fine. We can forget all about it."

She started to cry on the other end. My chest felt tight and I wanted to make it better for her. I was sorry that it happened too.

"I don't think we can be friends anymore," she ground out.

I paused, not sure what to say. "I'm sorry Rachel. I'm really sorry."

"I have to go now, Will. Thank you for calling." She hung up the phone.

***

I stood staring at the screen saver of my cell phone. Everything felt fucked up. How could I have handled the situation any better? Maybe I could have talked to her in person. Maybe that would have been better.

My phone rang and startled me out of my daze of thoughts. For a second I hoped that maybe she was calling me back. Maybe I'd ask her to dinner and we could talk.

It was Alex.

"Hey Will."

"What's up?"

"We can meet the guy tomorrow about buying more weed, at 8:00."

I nodded. "Okay."

"You all right?"

"Yeah. I'm fine. Are you all right?"

"Not really. Feeling overwhelmed about things with my mom, but when I pick you up tomorrow, we'll talk."

"Okay, Alex. We can talk then." I hung up the phone.

I went to dial Rachel's number again, but I hesitated on the last digit. I took a deep breath and decided not to press it. I placed my phone face down on the bedside table.

Tomorrow I would talk to her again. Her and I, we could work this thing out together. She needed to know that I liked her. For years, she was all I thought about. This couldn't be the way things ended between us.

Chapter
Fourteen

It was getting late and Alex was picking me up soon, so I walked outside to wait for him.

It was dusk and the moon was shining down through the clouds. I stared at it for a few minutes, listening to the sounds of the neighborhood. The air temperature was warm and I could hear the movement of traffic a few streets down from me. We lived on a pretty quiet street but our road was off the main boulevard, which was lined with retail stores, gas stations, and traffic lights. A dog barked in the distance and I turned my head to look toward the direction of the noise. The sidewalks in front of my house were crumbling. Garbage cans lined the street for pick-up first thing in the morning. I walked to the neighbors' yard and dragged Carol's garbage can to the curb, feeling bad for her with her boyfriend in jail and all. She really was in over her head with all those children.

I thought about Rachel, wishing things had played out differently. We had always been good friends to one another. We had good conversation; maybe we could have helped each other. I don't know. It seemed a waste to become that intimate with someone, and then have it all thrown away without even having a moment to talk about it fully. She was worried about what people thought of her, that they were judging her and labeling her too.

Just like my mother and just like Alex's mom.

I was trying to stay positive about it, thinking maybe she would come around once things settled down. I was hoping, anyway.

Alex pulled in down the street. I could tell his car from a mile away: He always drove slowly, with the music real loud.

He passed me with a deep grin on his face, leaning his elbow slightly out of the car window. Up the street, he turned around. As he came back, a few kids on bikes stopped on the sidewalk and watched him. The Chevy was a looker. Alex was lucky his father trusted him enough to give him his car.

Alex stopped and I opened up the door and looked inside.

"You're so ridiculous," I commented.

The kids on bikes pedaled by and one yelled, "Hey! Nice car, man."

"Hear that?" Alex said. It was just the encouragement that he needed. I rolled my eyes.

"Yeah, I heard that. They think you're cool." I laughed as I got into the vehicle.

Alex smirked. "Too cool for school, bro." He bumped his fist against mine and put the car in drive.

We drove a few minutes before Alex started to talk about where we were going.

"It's a frat house. Some rich kid's father owns a marijuana distribution facility out in Colorado. Apparently, they have acres and acres of marijuana plants at this kid's disposal. Good weed too; they use it for medicinal purposes."

He pulled off the main road and rounded the vehicle toward the off-campus housing.

"I've heard of this fraternity," I said. Average students, average parties, run-of-the-mill fraternity whose requirements to get in were that you couldn't be a scholar and you couldn't be a jock. It seemed pretty cool to me because I was neither of those things.

He parked the car on the street and we both got out of the vehicle in front of Kappa Delta V house. The house looked in disrepair: Garbage lined the flowerbeds and some of the porch railings were broken. The massive Victorian home had to be at least three floors, maybe even four, and needed a paint job.

I followed Alex around the back as he led me to the side door of the kitchen. A few kids were sitting around on the back porch, smoking cigarettes and talking. They didn't seem too interested in us, so we opened the door and walked into the house.

The kitchen was a mess; every counter space was full of dirty, piled-on dishes that no one seemed to ever clean.

"Hello?" Alex yelled. We both stared at each other. No one appeared so we continued to walk into the living room. A few guys were sitting on the couch watching football. One looked up at us and nodded.

"What's up?" he asked.

"Hey, we're looking for Parker. Any idea where he is?"

"Third floor," the boy replied.

"Cool, thanks."

Alex walked past the couches and entered the hallway leading to an enormous staircase to the second floor. During its prime, the staircase was probably really something to look at. The railings were spiraled mahogany; the stairs were wide and long. The carpet that had once been a thick, vibrant red was now dirty, stained, and fraying on its edges.

We walked up the stairs. Alex seemed calm and at ease about this interaction. My palms, conversely, were sweating and I could feel the tightness of apprehension spread across my shoulders. I wasn't sure if this was the right thing for me to do, but I really needed the money and Parker was the person to help.

We reached the second floor, rounded a corner, and continued walking down another hallway toward the staircase for the third floor. We passed one of the many bedrooms on the left when something caught my eye. Stopping, I looked into the room and watched as a kid around my age was taking a hit of something using a plastic bag attached to an oxygen tank. It looked so bizarre—I had never seen anything like it. My confusion must have shown on my face because one of the other students looked over at me.

"Do you want a hit?"

I looked at him. "What is it?"

"It's helium. Have you ever tried it?"

Alex popped his head into the doorway to see what I was staring at. "It's a whip it!" he said. "Dope. It basically makes you laugh and talk funny."

I shrugged, not wanting to appear stupid. "Oh yeah, yeah. I've heard of that before." *I have never heard of that before.*

"Ya gonna try it?" Alex asked.

I suddenly felt embarrassed. What if I did it wrong? What did it feel like? "Yeah, I guess so." I walked over to the kid who was holding the tank and looked at him.

"You put your mouth on this and suck it like you're sucking on a helium balloon."

I did what he told me. I sucked it in and held it. Then I let it out and instantly started giggling. I tried to talk to Alex but my voice was unrecognizable. Everyone in the room started laughing.

I walked back toward Alex, feeling like it was *the room* moving around me, and not me moving through the room. My body felt light and my heart was racing. "Thank you," I said to the student holding the tank, and my high-pitched girly voice sent Alex grasping for his stomach; I thought he was going to fall over. It felt good though—I wasn't nervous anymore about the transaction.

Alex walked out of the room, making his way toward the stairway. I followed him, my energy and confidence restored. We reached the third floor and knocked on bedroom doors. "Parker! Hey Parker!"

A door opened. "Come in here, man."

We entered the bedroom and Alex shook Parker's hand. "I'm Alex; this is Will."

"Hey what's up?" I reached out my hand and said hello.

Parker returned to his desk where he had been working.

"We're here to buy some weed," Alex said. "My friend Jonas knows you."

"Oh yeah, Jonas. He mentioned you would stop by." Parker waved us forward. "Come on over here and take a look." He hesitated and looked Alex and me over. "Do you guys go to school here?"

"No, I work for my father's business in town and Will is attending community college."

"Oh yeah, okay." Parker reached underneath his bunk bed and pulled out a suitcase. He opened it and revealed bags upon bags of neatly wrapped drug paraphernalia. Some had labels, some didn't. Some were very large, some were very small.

I was shocked at the variety. "Wow!"

"Nice, huh?" Parker stated.

"How much for five hundred?" Alex asked.

Parker picked up a larger bag of marijuana and tossed it to Alex. Alex sniffed its contents and smiled.

"Smells good, real good." He handed the bag of weed to me and I did the same, although I wouldn't know much of the difference. It did smell good, however, and it seemed like a lot of weed for five hundred dollars, more than my neighbors' bag.

I reached into my back pocket and pulled out the money. I handed it to Parker, who snatched it from my hand. He shut the suitcase firmly than placed it neatly back underneath his bed.

He turned around and faced us.

"Let's smoke, boys!"

Alex glanced over at me and smirked. Then we all sat down around a bong.

Easiest transaction I ever made.

Chapter
Fifteen

When I got home that evening, I immediately started to get to work. I did what Alex told me and divided the weed into small bags, placing them in a box underneath my bed. I told myself I would only do this one time, but I knew that was a lie.

It felt good, taking charge of my financial situation. Making friends was easy and there didn't seem to be huge risks involved. My father would be angry. He was the only deterrent that I felt, for my mother wouldn't have a clue what was happening. But my father…he would have to be dealt with. He was unlikely to let things go without punishment.

I thought about what the gypsy said. Was I doing the right thing, was I checking the right box? It felt like there was a clock ticking somewhere and I wasn't sure when my time would be up, as if I would turn the corner one day and that would be the end of me. It seemed an irrational fear to have, knowing that the gypsy lady was peculiar, but her threat still sat with me. I tried to shrug those feelings off.

I couldn't care enough about the consequences. I knew that I could be arrested. I also knew, according to the gypsy, that my life could be in danger. I understood that it was illegal what I was doing, but that didn't seem to matter either. It was hard to explain why I was getting involved in this…but my friends needed me. They called me, they invited me places and to parties; everyone was so nice to me. Besides, I had always looked after my mother and I had always tried to do the things that my father wanted. What about me? I never thought about myself. Right now, I wanted to belong somewhere. I wanted friends. It took the loneliness away. It gave me the confidence to move forward in my life.

Parker invited us to an initiation party at the Kappa house the next day. I was hesitant to go alone, so I invited Alex to come. I wondered if Alex would have some good advice for me, about Rachel. I wished I could feel peaceful about my situation with her, but she avoided me at every possible corner. I think she was ashamed with what had happened between us. If we talked about it, I knew we could sort it out, but she needed to open that box for herself. I couldn't do it for her.

Alex seemed lost in his thoughts as he drove. The car was silent as I watched him, his eyes unsure as he bit on his lip, grappling with what was happening to his life and his family. I could feel his anxiety and wanted so badly to help him, especially after all the help he's given me throughout the years.

"My parents are getting divorced," he said.

I knew that this was likely to be the case. It still struck me hard because I always looked up to Alex's parents as model people whose family was the most perfect I had come to know.

Alex took a deep breath. "My mother and Angie want to get married."

His words seemed more normal now, about his mother and Angie. "My mom and Angie" seemed to roll off his tongue as if they were already a unit, a couple that we'd known for a long time now.

"She's okay, my mom. I love her; she really is the best mom. It's just so confusing."

"You seem more accepting of it now, though," I brought up.

Alex's face became soft and concerned. "I think back on her life and I could remember that there was always a certain unhappiness about her. She was happy but sad at the same time. It's hard to explain."

I nodded. I didn't know how to respond, so I didn't, but I understood that feeling of sadness that Alex talked about.

"That sentiment is familiar," I managed quietly. Alex looked at me with thoughtful eyes. "I would give anything to have a semi-normal mother, Alex. If this is the worst of your problems, it's really not that bad. Your mom deserves to be happy." I paused. "Are you okay, Alex?"

"I'm a little worried for her. People are assholes. It's embarrassing and all, to think about your mom with a woman, but mostly I don't want people to be mean to her. I can handle a little backlash. I'll just tell people to fuck off, but I worry about her."

"Your mom is a very strong woman," I said with a smile. "She's badass, Alex. She's not afraid to tell people to fuck off either."

"Ha! Yeah, I guess you're right."

I placed my hand on Alex's shoulder and squeezed tight. "It's going to be okay...and besides, who wants to live a boring life anyway?"

"I guess so."

"She's going to have to adjust to people judging her and labeling her in a certain way. I learned this a long time ago with my mother."

Alex looked at me with full understanding. "My mother will overcome this. She's part of a minority now; she's going to have to learn to be stronger; she'll need to develop a tougher skin."

"Maybe we need to start thinking about things in a different way too. Think more positive thoughts, like being gay is super cool and unique, and it's obvious you want your mom to be happy. Don't attach so much fear to what's happening. Be open to it and positive—you are anyway. Open the box and move forward with love for your mother, and see if that helps you."

Alex paused in thought. "That's really good advice, Will. When did you get so insightful?"

We both started laughing.

"I have no idea, but I care about you and your mom and I don't want to see you suffer over this. It's really silly and not that *huge* of a deal. The people who will understand will gravitate toward your mom, and the ones who don't will weed themselves out. Those people won't matter to her anymore."

Will nodded and I could tell he was relieved. "Thanks for listening, Will. I really needed to talk with someone."

"Yeah, no problem buddy. I'm here if you need me, anytime." We bumped our fists together, a thing we always did ever since we were young.

Alex reached over to the stereo and turned up the volume. "I wonder if there will be any hot chicks here tonight."

I glanced over at Alex and thought about asking him for advice regarding Rachel, but then I reconsidered. He had a lot of experience with girls, but none of it had anything to do with real love. "I'm sure there will be plenty of girls, playa," I teased.

Alex smiled proudly. "I know you get annoyed about that," he said, "but it makes me feel better."

"Your ego is bruised right now, that's all it is. You're trying to overcompensate for what's happening with your mom. To be honest, it's a little childish. You're like a two-year-old screaming, 'Look at me, look at me. Someone, anyone...pay attention to me.'"

"Shut the hell up. I do *not* act like that."

"Yes, sometimes you do."

"Whatever man. Once a playa, always a playa."

We pulled up to Parker's house. A crowd had formed and music was playing. I nodded to the beat as I stepped out of the vehicle thinking tonight was going to be a fun night. Several girls walked past giggling, smiling. One girl turned back and said, "Heyyy." I recognized them from high school.

"Ladies." I smiled.

Alex stepped out onto the sidewalk and stopped the girls from moving along. "You girls going to the party?"

"We were thinking about it," one girl commented.

"Why don't we go inside and find ourselves a nice spot and get to know each other a little better?" Alex offered.

The girls easily followed us as we walked into the house, stopping at the whip it room. I popped my head inside to say hello to the guys. There they were, doing the hits off the tank, just like last time.

"Hey! Looks like you guys never moved," I commented.

One guy started laughing. "I'm pretty sure we did, but…maybe we didn't."

"I think I'm failing fitness education," said the other boy.

"How the fuck you fail fitness?" said his roommate.

"I don't know, I'm just saying I haven't moved from this room and I'm pretty sure I'm failing something."

I turned and whispered to Madi, "Have you ever had a hit of this before?"

She smiled back. "Yeah, my older brother let me try it one time when I was visiting him at college. It was fun."

I looked over at Alex. He nodded at me so I asked, "Hey, you guys mind if we take a hit? We've got some weed we could smoke too."

"Yeah, no problem, come on in and lock the door."

We piled into the bedroom and Alex shut the door behind him. The girls stood in line first and took hits off the tank. Immediately they started to giggle. Becka got a little dizzy and sat cross-legged on the floor and the other girls followed suit. I broke up some weed and rolled a nice-looking joint, lit it, and passed it around. The radio was playing and the roommates were still arguing about failing fitness class at school. Out of the corner of my eye I could see Alex starting to kiss Carey.

"Oh hey, we still need to find Parker," I announced, breaking up the party.

"Fuck Parker," Alex said as he continued to kiss her.

"Parker's down in the basement," one of the roommates mentioned.

"The basement?" I asked.

"Yeah, you got any money?" he replied. "You might want to bring some."

I looked at him confused. "Money for what?"

"To gamble," he said.

I assumed the boys were playing poker. I wasn't a card guy, but I was curious anyway. I looked at Alex. "You coming?"

"I'll catch up with you guys later."

I nodded. "Come on, girls." I reached over and smacked one of the roommate's shoulders as we were leaving. "Thanks a lot buddy."

We walked downstairs to the bottom floor. I checked several doors in the hallway hoping that one of them would lead to the basement. The house was crowded with people and the music was loud, making it hard to hear anyone.

My final attempt at the last door hit magic. The door sprung open and led to a dusty stairwell surrounded by brick and mortar, a few cobwebs and some screaming and yelling coming from down below.

I glanced back at the girls, hoping they may want to stop me from walking down those stairs, but they didn't seem deterred in any way. I continued down and when we reached the bottom, my stomach dropped.

I couldn't believe my eyes.

Chapter

Sixteen

I stood on the last stair in the basement, holding on to a low beam that hung from the ceiling. Many students crowded the space between the landing and the far end of the room. It was hard to see, but there was no mistake as to what was going on. I could hear the dogs growling and I could see some of the students jumping up and down as they cheered.

It was a dogfight, the kind you only hear about but never actually get a chance to witness.

I felt disgusted. I couldn't imagine feeling joy or excitement over the demise or pain and suffering of an animal...and here I was, watching so many students enjoying what was happening. I didn't understand it. I turned to the girls and told them to go back upstairs. They both shook their heads no, and continued to walk past me toward the crowd that circled the fighting ring. Several cages were scattered along the walls of the basement and random bags of dog food were placed haphazardly here and there. Many bags were ripped into, as if mice had gotten into them. The basement was dark and cloudy; some students were smoking, which made it even more difficult to see clearly.

I noticed a few cages had dogs in them. Pit bulls. I knelt down to one cage and the dog nearly took my hand off as I reached in to pet him. I stood up, angry. No animal should live like that, in fear of what was to come.

Across the room, Parker stood on a chair looking over the crowd and into the fighting ring. He waved dollar bills as he screamed at the animals.

The muscles in my jaw were tight and a beating throb in my temple was about to explode.

I pushed students to the side as I muscled my way through the crowd toward Parker. Blood was noticeably splattered along the concrete flooring, some dried and old. I reached up to Parker and tried to pull him off his chair. He was irritated by my persistent tugging but stepped down anyway.

"What the fuck Will? I'm busy right now. We can do business later." Parker spoke but his eyes never left the fighting ring.

"This is disgusting! Are you in charge of this? Did you do this?" I yelled.

I heard one of the dogs whimper and turned to look. The animal's face was covered with blood; its leg was badly hurt. Its ear had been lopped off and fear flashed in the dog's eyes. The opposing dog lunged at him and grabbed it by the neck with his teeth, tossing the dog back and forth on the floor. Finally, the dog didn't move.

Parker started to cheer. "Yeah, yeah mother fucker. Payday is here!"

I stared at him in disbelief. He turned to me and shook my shoulders with excitement. My mouth dropped open and with the smell of death in the room, I leaned over and vomited on the floor.

Parker looked at me, revolted. I stood tall and wiped my mouth and glared back at him.

"You're a fucking pussy," he stated as he attempted to stand back on the chair.

I kicked the chair out from underneath him and pulled my arm back, smashing Parker in the face with my fist, catching him off guard.

Blood dripped from his nose as he stepped back from me. "What the fuck, Will?"

It felt so good to punch him, and it was hard for me to restrain myself. I wanted to keep hurting him, to make him feel pain.

"You're a fucking dirt bag!" I screamed as I lunged at him again.

Parker punched me hard on my mouth, splitting my lip. My head snapped back as I stumbled over the concrete and landed on the floor. My brain was rattled and I couldn't see clearly. Madi was suddenly pulling me up, forcing me toward the stairway.

"Come on, Will! It's not worth it! Let's get out of here," she yelled.

I wiped my lip dry. As I turned to leave, I saw a puppy sitting in a cage underneath the basement stairs. I looked around me; the students were busy exchanging money. Parker was still yelling.

"Don't ever fucking come back to this house again, Will."

I ignored him and focused on the puppy. I leaned over to Madi and told her to stand behind me, to block anyone's view. "I'm going to take the puppy," I whispered in her ear. Her eyes were wide and she nodded as she tried her best to cover me.

I crawled on the floor underneath the stairwell and opened the cage. The puppy was scared and stood in the far corner away from me. I reached down and picked some popcorn off the floor that a student must have dropped. I held it out in front of the puppy and she licked it. Slowly she approached me and I reached in and grabbed her. She didn't fight but snuggled herself warmly underneath my shirt.

"Run Madi!" I yelled. She ran up the stairs and I followed her. Becka was already at the top, holding the door for us.

"Where's Alex?" I asked breathlessly.

"He's at the car."

I walked through the house, the two girls behind me and a puppy underneath my T-shirt. When I reached the vehicle, Alex was in the driver's seat, Carey was sitting in between us, and the two girls climbed into the back. I pulled out the puppy.

"What the hell happened to you, and why do you have a puppy?" Alex asked.

I looked at him and smiled. "This is for my mama."

Alex didn't ask any more questions.

Chapter

Seventeen

My house was eerily quiet as I ran up the stairs to the front door and placed my puppy in the small crate on the porch. I opened the door and walked inside.

"Mom?" I spoke into the silence and stood still on the carpet, waiting for her to respond. Instantly I had a sinking feeling that something was wrong. I noticed an empty bottle of cabernet on the counter and a nauseating wave of dread overwhelmed me. I tried to convince myself that everything was fine here, but my legs were shaking.

"MOM!" I yelled. I walked through the house and opened the doors to the bedrooms. My voice echoed off the walls. Nobody else was here. My mother was nowhere to be found.

My limbs couldn't move fast enough. I went to the window where she always stood, staring at the house next door. I could see the lights on and guessed that the neighbors were still up, which was no big surprise. Maybe Carol saw her.

I jogged down the hallway toward the back door and shoved it open. I jumped off the porch and made it to the neighbor's front door in seconds. I pounded loudly.

Carol came to the door with a toddler on her hip and a cigarette in her hand. "Yeah? What do you want?"

"I can't find my mother," I gasped.

Carol looked at me for a second then placed the toddler on the ground. "Go find your sister," she stated as she patted her softly on her diaper. Carol opened the door and stepped out onto the front porch.

"I haven't seen her today," she said, concerned.

"What the fuck. She never leaves the house! Where would she go?" I could feel my heart race and desperately looked at Carol for answers.

"There was a fire earlier, down the street. The road was full of fire engines and police vehicles. Perhaps she was worried and took a walk down that way to check it out." Carol pointed toward the main intersection. Three family homes lined the road that ran along the main street and around the corner.

"Okay, thanks Carol." I jumped off the porch.

"Hey! Do you want me to call the police?" she yelled after me.

"*No!*" I responded. No police. It's not what I wanted. I wanted to find my mother safe and give her the puppy. I thought this was going to be a great night for her and I. My lungs burned as I blazed past our house and toward the main road. It was only a quarter mile but the anxiety made it hard to breathe.

It was obvious which house had caught fire. The upper floor windows were blackened from smoke and a fire truck was still outside. Nearby, a few people were corralled together while one woman was crying about the damage to her home.

There was no sign of my mother.

I stopped on the sidewalk and turned in circles, looking around me at every angle of the street. "Which fucking way would she go?"

I didn't know what to do. Maybe I could call my dad, but it was late. Maybe she called a cab again and was off someplace I would never be able to find her. She could be anywhere, without any idea what she was doing or who she was dealing with.

I felt a panic attack coming. I couldn't catch my breath. It was 11:30 PM. The night was dark and cold. I closed my eyes and prayed for help.

I ran to the fire truck and spoke to one of the firemen. "Hey, sorry to bother you...but my mom is missing."

The fireman looked up at me, his face dirty from the ashes and his eyes tired. "Your mom is missing?"

"Yes. She's missing. She may have been here, watching you put out the fire. She's about this tall." I held my hand up to the center of my chest. "She has brown shaggy hair, and it's possible that she might have been wearing her pajamas. She has a medical disorder and I'm really worried about her."

The fireman took a deep breath and picked up his walkie talkie. I could hear static come over the speaker and then he spoke into the intercom. "This is Cooper here, requesting Lieutenant Johnson."

More static then, "Hey Cooper. This is Johnson. What's your status?"

"I have a young man standing with me who says he's looking for his mother. She has a medical issue and she seems to have gone missing." I watched the firefighter look down at his watch then up at the house.

There was silence over the radio. "Sorry, we have no report of an older woman in distress. Maybe check with the police station."

158

Before the firefighter could reply, I yelled my thanks and ran back toward the house. I grabbed my mother's keys off of the counter and jumped into her car. I put the key in the ignition and pressed on the gas, but the only noise I could hear was a loud ticking coming through the dashboard.

"Come on!" I yelled, slamming on the steering wheel. I tried to start the car again and I felt a quick jolt, but then nothing. Just a soft ticking of the engine that wouldn't ignite. *Piece of shit.*

I looked down at the gas meter. The car was on empty. Frustrated, I ran back around the house toward our shed and grabbed a gas can and shook it. I lifted it toward the streetlight, hoping to gauge how much remained. Maybe there was a quarter gallon of gas left. *Please, God, work.* The rusted gas cap of my mother's old car was stiff and tight as I twisted it and placed the hose directly into the tank. I watched it empty.

Throwing it aside, I hopped back into the driver's seat and waited. Tapping my fingers on the key, I closed my eyes one last time. I stepped lightly on the gas while turning the ignition. A slow murmur began to hum and then a loud rattle and finally a burst of energy. The engine turned.

"YESSSS!" I could feel my stomach relax as I drove to the nearest gas station and added more fuel.

Once fueled up, I traveled down the neighborhood adjacent to ours; up and down the streets I drove looking for something, anything that might be a sign of my mother.

There was a different life on the streets at 1:00 AM—a lonely life where people seemed to wonder the sidewalks alone, either looking for drugs or having no place to live. Tortured thoughts filled me; the fear of where my mother could be was almost paralyzing.

I couldn't do this alone. I had to go to the police.

I drove toward the station, thinking of the gypsy's words. Maybe it was my mother's life that was in danger. Like Molly, my lost dog, maybe I would never see my mother again. The thought simultaneously terrified me and gave me peace, in a weird way. Because of the gypsy's premonition, I was always thinking about dying and worrying about when my time was going to be up, always looking over my shoulder and wondering if I was doing the right things. Maybe she had it wrong all along. Maybe it was my mother she was feeling.

It was possible that if something horrible happened to my mother, they would take her away from me, place her in someone else's care—someone more capable. It would be out of my hands then, caring for my mother. I wasn't sure if I would be upset about that, but I felt guilty for even thinking it or feeling that way.

Please, God, forgive me.

I walked into the police station and stopped at the front desk.

"My mother is missing," I said. "Is there someone here who could help me?"

The woman behind the desk looked tired and bored. With a toothpick in her mouth she motioned toward a group of people sitting in a waiting room.

"Over there," she said. "You need to get in line and an officer will be with you shortly."

I looked over at the line, about twenty people before me. I closed my eyes tightly and took a deep breath.

This is a nightmare.

Chapter

Eighteen

I called my aunt and we waited together at the station, until 6:00 AM. It was a toss-up between calling my aunt or my dad, but I settled for Aunt Bev, who was going to be less judgmental on my mom, but more aggressive on me.

"This is completely irresponsible, Will. What do you do at night anyway? You go out, have fun with your friends while your poor mother is alone and waiting for you?"

I never had to wonder where my mother got the ability to make me feel guilty, because Aunt Bev was just like her in that way.

"You know Bev, I could use a little break every once in a while. You never come around anymore. I'm not sure what you expect from me, but I am young and would like to have a life. It's not easy to be with my mother, you know. It could be miserable at times, if I'm completely honest."

Aunt Bev looked around the room as if someone might be able to overhear us. "If you feel this way, why don't you call me? I would come, Will. All you need to do is ask me. I don't have telepathy, Will."

"I *have* called you, and if you were around more, you would see for yourself that she's not doing well."

Aunt Bev lowered her eyes. It felt good to make her feel bad, to give it right back to her.

"How's the drinking?" she asked.

I let out a deep exhale and looked away from her.

"What about your father? Is he around at all? He might be able to help you once in a while, at least with the house and in the yard."

"I don't want to bring my father into this. He has enough on his plate."

"That's your problem, Will. You don't want to ask for any help. If you don't ask for help, you're not going to receive it. You need to communicate your needs better so that your father and I could sit down with you and your mom and we could figure out a better system. When we find your mother, we can talk about doing that."

If we find her.

A police officer approached us from behind a desk. "They took an older woman earlier today to the emergency room at the University Medical Center. She was very confused. It's possible that it is your mother."

I grabbed the officer by the shoulders, relieved. "Thank you! Thank you very much!"

My aunt insisted that she follow me, which was fine because she was always helpful with the medical doctors. I was able to speed through town, every light turning green just as I approached it. The parking lot was full at the hospital, except for one space up front, which seemed to be meant just for me.

The emergency room was crowded with patients and people waiting, so I bypassed them and walked up and down the hallways looking for her. I asked one nurse if she knew where she could be but she only pushed me aside and told me to check with registration.

I was starting to get frustrated, but as I was about to leave the floor, I heard her voice.

"How do you think it started?" she asked.

"What, ma'am?" the intern asked politely.

"The fire, of course."

I walked into a room and looked at my mother as she sat on the bed. An intern was taking her blood pressure and checking her temperature.

"Mom!" I said.

"William!" She tried to stand up, but I made her sit back down. "Did you see what happened? There was a fire and smoke, and people were screaming."

"Why did you leave without telling me, Mom? I was really worried. I had no idea where you were!"

My mother's face was smudged with smoke dust and her hair looked gray and sandy with ash. Her clothing was saturated with the smell of smoke and she had a small cut above her eyebrow.

"Oh William, but the *fire*."

Just as my mother spoke, my aunt stepped into the room behind me. My mother's face became rigid and her lips pursed, ready to combat us over her behavior. I refrained from becoming more frustrated than I already was. I was happy she was okay and that we were together. She wasn't lost—that was the most important thing.

"Linda, we sat at the police station all night while the officers spent their time and energy looking for you. Do you realize how much time we wasted today, when all of this could have been avoided?"

I sat next to my mother on the bed and placed my arm around her shoulder. The intern nodded at me.

"She's okay. She was a little scared and confused but she's not seriously injured."

I wiped the worry away from my eyes and laughed nervously, relieved that these long hours were finally over. "Thank you," I said to the intern.

"Yes, thank you," my aunt added. My mother was no stranger to the hospital. She once spent a week in the psych unit because she refused to eat. I explained to the doctors that she had grown up rough, and that food was often taken from her for bad behavior. I thought she was having some sort of flashback. My aunt had also been there; she was technically my mother's guardian, even though she didn't live with us. The doctors didn't know this; this was just between the three of us. We tried to explain my mother's behavior to the doctors, but they put her in the psych ward anyway. They force-fed her until she finally gave in and started to eat on her own. When they released her, she didn't remember what had happened. She was good at blocking out memories, if she didn't want to deal with them.

The intern stood up. "Dr. Forrest has already checked in on her. He's cleared her to go home whenever you are ready." Dr. Forrest was one of her medical doctors. It was fortunate for us that he worked part-time in the emergency room.

My mother looked up at the intern. "Do you know how it started?" she asked again.

"It's okay, Mom, the fire's out now. We're going to go home soon." I nodded at the nurse and she walked out of the room.

"You scared the hell out of us," my aunt hollered.

"God, can you keep it down?" My aunt could be so annoying at times, and not helpful.

"I don't need your attitude, Will." My aunt's keys jingled around as she searched for them in her purse.

"It's fine, Aunt Bev. I've got it from here. I appreciate you coming out and helping."

Aunt Bev looked at my mother sternly. "Things are going to change soon, Linda. Will and I had a long talk and this type of behavior's not going to happen anymore. Do you understand?"

I rolled my eyes and turned my head so my aunt couldn't see my annoyance.

My mother stared at her blankly. "Okay then, goodbye."

Aunt Bev paused with frustration and then loudly walked out of the room.

My mother looked down at her feet. "It was exciting," she whispered as she leaned into my chest.

"Oh really?" I laughed. "That's what you think? It was exciting!" My mother shrugged and batted her eyes at me. A trick she taught me when I was young.

"It's not going to work, Mom. I'm really upset about this. You could have been hurt."

"William? How do you think it started?" It was the third time she asked.

"It was unfortunate, Mom." I shook my head back and forth. "Someone had been smoking," I replied. I didn't know the truth of that, but I needed to give her an answer.

My mother looked disappointed. She seemed to accept this explanation and didn't ask again.

It was a silent ride home. I slowed down the car as we passed the house on the corner, the windows still black with smoke.

"They probably need things now, like furniture and clothing. Maybe we can donate something to them," she mentioned.

"That's a really nice idea, Mom. We should definitely do that."

My eyes were heavy. I thought about the puppy. I decided to wait until later to give her to my mother. We had enough excitement for one day.

"William?"

"Yeah, Mom."

"What happened to your face?" I completely forgot about my face. I looked in the rear view mirror and inspected my fat lip, which showed signs of dried blood and bruising around my chin.

"It's a long story, Mom. I'll explain it to you tomorrow."

My mother leaned back into the seat and folded her arms. "You interrogate me over leaving the house like I'm some kind of child, and here you are, punched in the face."

I couldn't believe her attitude. "Yeah, that's right, Mom. I had a rough night tonight. I was in a fight with some asshole and then I came home hoping to find you and share some good news, but instead, I had to run around the streets looking for you, scared, and now I'm completely exhausted and I don't want to talk about how or why I got punched in the face!" I was losing my temper and wasn't about to let her exhaust me anymore. "I want to go home in peace and quiet, and I don't want to talk about it anymore. Can we manage that for today? Please?"

My mother rolled her eyes. She kept her mouth shut and for the first time in a long time, it felt good to lay it on her. Sometimes she was too much to take. She

169

didn't know how lucky she was, how much I sacrificed for her.

Chapter
Nineteen

I felt better the next afternoon. My mother was rested and seemed to remember everything that happened the night before.

"I know we've talked about this, Mom. It's very important that you listen to me and understand. If you need to go somewhere, I will go with you. If I'm not around, then you at least need to tell me where you're heading."

My mother walked around the kitchen in her bathrobe and coffee cup in hand. "We need fire extinguishers. We need fire alarms." She continued into the living room, looking up at the ceiling. She raised her hands in attempt to press the button on the circular alarm. A loud warning rang through the house, indicating that the batteries were working perfectly.

"See, Mom. We have an alarm. Everything is okay in the house." I opened the cabinet underneath the sink to show her the fire extinguisher. "See? This is where the fire extinguisher is." My mother looked at me, still. I walked to her and led her to the chair. I knelt in front of her and took her hands.

"Mom, I need to talk to you. Can you listen to me for a minute?" She was ready to interrupt me but her eyes soften and she let out a deep breath. "I know that you're worried about things. I know that you feel scared. I've got something for you that I think will help you."

"What is it dear? What do you have?" she asked.

"Stay right here! I'll be right back."

I stood and walked out of the living room, down the hall to my bedroom. I opened the door and knelt by the dog crate. Lola came out, reluctantly. I picked her up and held her high.

"I promise you girl, you and my mother need each other. You will help her and she will help you." I kissed her head and snuggled her against my neck. "Be a good girl, Lola."

I walked back into the living room and held the puppy close to my chest as I sat down next to my mother. I lifted her slightly so my mother could see her.

"Oh, William. What did you do?" she asked. My mother's face crumbled with adoration. Her arms stretched out and she gently took Lola and held her against her stomach.

"I rescued her, Mom. Her name is Lola. I found her last night. She was locked in a cage and they were going to raise her to dogfight. They were going to kill her."

My mother wiped tears from her eyes with the back of her hand. "What do you mean, they were going to kill her? Who was going to kill her?" she asked angrily.

"It's a long story, but I was at a frat party last night and they had a fighting ring. Another pit bull died; it was awful to see." I swallowed. "I couldn't stand what was happening. She really needs to be loved and watched over. Isn't she so sweet?"

"Oh Will," my mother managed, "is that why you were punched in the face?"

"Partly."

My mother talked to Lola gently and stroked her belly. She was sleepy and snuggled in warmly with my mother. For the next hour they sat together, nestling and whispering.

I could feel a certain amount of worry subside. The dog and my mom would take good care of each other.

***

I spent the rest of my morning organizing the weed that I had remaining from Parker. I knew that I screwed up in a big way. I had no one to turn to now for the drugs. Maybe it was for the best. I could sell the rest of what I had and then it would be over.

But then I thought about the helium tanks. Maybe I could get one of those and bring it to the next party. That would be cool—then I could let my friends take hits off the tank and they would think that I was important.

I picked up the phone and dialed Alex's number.

"Hey, what's up?" he answered.

"How'd it go last night, with Carey?" I asked.

"She's called me twice today," he replied.

"Oh, she must like you."

"But seriously, why do girls do that? I was planning to ask her out again tonight, but she's taking all the fun out of it. She's making it too easy. Hey, do you want to double? I can ask for that girl's number, Becka?"

"Nah, I can't man. My mom was missing last night and I found her in the emergency room. Plus, I have the puppy. I don't want to leave them tonight. It's all very new."

"Holy shit! What do you mean she went missing?"

"It's an annoying story and I don't want to talk about it. Anyway, I want to know where I can buy a helium tank."

"Why?"

"I don't know. We can bring it to the party on Saturday. I'm really low on weed and I fucked up with Parker."

"Yeah, he's super pissed at you."

"I know, but I thought maybe I could do that for everyone. Bring a tank."

"I think it's pretty easy to get one. You buy them at a party store, where they sell balloons."

"No shit?"

"Yeah, no shit."

"Okay, cool. I'm gonna do that then." I didn't realize it would be so easy. I said goodbye and hung up the phone. I grabbed the car keys and started for the door.

"Hey, Mom, I need to run out. Are you going to be okay here with the dog for a while?"

My mother's smile was proud. I walked over to Lola and nuzzled her soft rolls. The small patches of black around her ankles and eyes were distinctive. "Oh honey, isn't she just beautiful?"

"She's cute, Mom. I'm going to stop at the pet store and buy her a few things and some chew sticks. Do you need anything?"

My mother jumped at the opportunity. "Let me give you some money. You can buy her one of those little beds and maybe a coat. What about a leash? Do we have a leash?"

"I'll grab one for her."

"And food, Will. She needs food."

"Okay, Mom. I'll get her what she needs."

My mother placed the dog on the floor and watched her waddle around exploring her new home and surroundings.

I left the house and drove downtown to the pet store, which was conveniently located right next door to the party store. I walked up and down the aisles, getting lost in the vastness of dog and animal products. I filled my cart with the necessities and went to the checkout. A school friend of mine worked there.

"Hey what's up, Mack? How are you?"

"Wow, you're buying the motherlode," Mack replied. "Hey, do you have a coupon?" I must have made a face because he reached underneath the counter and slipped me a twenty percent off coupon from the newspaper.

"Thanks," I replied. "I owe you one."

"Yeah, no problem." Mack started to ring up my purchase.

Several girls entered the store. I tried not to stare but I couldn't believe it—Rachel was there. I hadn't spoken to her since that phone call, which was months ago.

She slowed her pace and lingered for a minute at the exit door. She looked good. She looked beautiful, actually. I grabbed my bag of things and walked to where she was standing.

"Hey Rach," I said with a smile.

"Hey Will," she replied.

I stared at her briefly. She didn't run from me. I figured that was a good sign.

"How are you?" I asked. "I haven't seen you since the end of the school year."

"Yeah, I know. I worked all summer at the Lobster Bake restaurant down by the shore, and then I went away to school in Boston. This is actually my first time back home; I have a few weeks' vacation."

"Boston! Wow! That's really great, Rachel. I'm glad you decided to go away to school after all." I paused and took a breath. "It feels really good to see you again."

177

Her face softened into a beautiful smile. She seemed more relaxed, more confident and she seemed glad to see me too.

"Hey, I know this might be awkward, but maybe I could take you to dinner tomorrow night? There's a party we could go to afterward. It should be a good time. You could catch up with some of your old friends." I looked at her expectantly. She was processing my words, probably had a list of pros and cons in her mind, but she nodded.

"Yeah, sure Will. I would like that. It would be good for us to talk."

When she said yes, my heart leapt inside me. I could feel a great sense of guilt and closure escape the cells of my body.

"Cool. Okay then, I'll call you tomorrow. I'll pick you up, say around 8:00?"

"Great!"

I walked through the electric door entrance and out into the parking lot. At the car's trunk, I shoved the bags over my golf clubs. I was happy. I was elated, actually. Those negative feelings I held about how things ended between us were gone now. Maybe this would be a new beginning, at least for a friendship between her and I. Maybe we could date.

I was hopeful.

I jogged back toward the party store and walked to the counter. A kid a little younger than me was working the desk.

"Hey, how are you?" I asked.

"What can I do for you?" The clerk was staring at his cell phone. He eventually looked up in my face and stood down off the chair he was sitting on.

"Hey, yeah, I was told that I could buy a helium tank here?" I was nervous for some reason. It seemed illegal, what I was about to do, but it wasn't. The clerk gave me a knowing smirk.

"Do you have a license?"

"Yes," I replied.

The clerk slid over a piece of paper. "Fill this out."

I looked at the form. It was basic stuff: my name, phone number, address.

I filled out the paperwork while the clerk went into the back room and returned with a small helium tank.

"Do you have anything bigger?" I asked. The clerk shrugged at me but went back to the storage room again and returned with a bigger tank.

"Thank you. I appreciate it." I paid the clerk and gave him my license and information. He gave me my change and I picked up the tank and walked out of the store.

Easy breezy. Just like that.

Chapter
Twenty

The radio was up and my windows were down as the cool wind hit my face. I drove through the streets back home, taking the long way, feeling the music move me. I felt high, but I wasn't. *Happy* was the word.

The deli down the street had amazing grinders so I stopped and picked up dinner. Tonight was a good night to watch a movie, snuggle with Lola, and chill out. I was looking forward to tomorrow, to my date with Rachel and to the party.

Good things were going to come out of my mother, I had faith. When I unloaded the bags onto the kitchen table, she dove into them, removing every item and showing Lola all of her new pretty things.

"Look Lola, a ball." My mother tossed the yellow ball across the floor and Lola ran from it.

"She's probably a little too frightened still," my mother laughed. "Oh, Lola. Look at your tiny bed." The corner of the living room was a perfect place, and my mother dropped Lola's bed onto the floor. Lola immediately started to bite the fabric and pull at the material. My mother scolded her but continued to be amused by the puppy's behavior.

As my mother was distracted, I took the opportunity to bring the helium tank through the back door and into my bedroom. She didn't notice my departure, her joy untouchable. I was not regretful of my decision to take the dog. It was the perfect thing to do.

I placed the helium tank next to my bed, along with a face mask I had purchased. I'd seen some kids use one, alleging that it gets you higher.

Returning to the living room, my mother and I sat down for dinner, although my mind was on Rachel.

Dinner felt normal. The energy in the entire house had magically changed, by one tiny little addition. We watched a movie, with Lola sleeping in between us. It was the first night in a long time that my mother didn't stand at the window, didn't ask questions about the neighbors, didn't talk about the fire. She sat peacefully, her hand on Lola's back, occasionally bending down to kiss her.

When the movie was over, we took Lola outside to pee. She managed to listen perfectly and came back when I called her. I picked her up and placed her in her crate.

"Good night, baby girl." My mother bent down to Lola one last time before she went to bed. She looked at me. "Oh sweetheart, she's so beautiful. Thank you for her. Thank you so much."

I opened my arms and hugged her for a long moment. Stepping back, she looked into my face. "Things are going to get better now, Will. I promise." My mother smiled brightly.

"I love you, Linda. You don't need to worry."

My mother laughed and slapped my arm playfully. "Don't call me that," she scolded then kissed me on my forehead. "Good night Will."

"Good night, Mom."

After a shower, I retreated to my room and locked the door. Sitting on my bed, the covers around me, I looked at the helium tank. I didn't want to bring the tank to the party, not knowing how to use it. I put the mask over my head and pretended to take a hit of the helium.

I did this several times then turned on the tank.

A soft whistle escaped the nozzle and I knew that it was on. I lifted the mask to my face and inhaled deeply.

I felt my body float back onto the bed and then, the lights went out.

Everything was dark.

***

It stayed this way for what felt like hours. I thought I was sleeping. I didn't feel pain. I didn't feel anything.

I could hear the dog cry. Softly. She whimpered. I wanted to go to her, but it was still dark.

"Will. Will. Wake up. Wake up."

The voice felt distant, but I could tell that it was my mother.

"Will! Please, Will. Wake up!"

She was crying and scared; her voice sounded frantic.

At first I thought I was in a bad dream. I could see some light through the darkness, so I walked toward it.

"Please, Will!" she wailed.

I could see her now, lying on top of my body, clinging to my shirt, she lay her face on my chest and sobbed.

"What just happened?" I asked. "What happened, Mom? Mom! Look at me, answer me! What did I do?"

I spoke but no sound came from me. All I could do was watch as she lay on me and cried. I felt helpless. Where was I? What was going on?

Then, the thought entered my mind. A terrifying, unwelcome thought.

I was dead.

There was a pull on my body, as if I were magnetized and surrounded by a ring of iron metal. I fought it, staying over my bed, trying desperately to get closer to my mother, to cross back over onto the other side. But the pull wouldn't let me. Where would I go? Where would it take me?

My heart wrenched and I screamed with panic, "Please, Mom! Help me! Please, I'm so sorry. I will do better, I promise, I won't let you down. Please!"

I watched the police come; they confiscated my drugs and helium tank. My mother roamed aimlessly around the house, clinging Lola against her chest, as the EMTs came to my bed and checked my pulse, removing the mask from my face.

They declared a time of death, moved me to a stretcher, and placed a white sheet over my body. I watched Mom struggle, her eyes filled with tears, her voice lost within her throat, incapable of speaking—her mind in complete shock, as was mine, that I had just died.

There was nothing I could do but watch.

My father was called; quickly he arrived and talked to the police. He tried to console my mother the best he could. Alex came to my bedroom and stood in my doorway, lost.

The pull was too strong and I was too weak to resist. I closed my eyes and felt the weightlessness as I began to float into a space that I was unsure of. I fell back and finally let myself go.

Chapter

Twenty-One

Big Joe sat at the back of the party, a stack of red plastic solo cups tucked under his arm and a keg tap in his hand. Alex went to him and sat down next to the bar as Big Joe handed him a cup of beer. Alex stared at him blankly. I watched their interaction.

"You sure you want to be here, man? It's a tough gig what happened with Will. Maybe you should go home."

Alex sucked down his beer and threw the cup across the room. I realized he wasn't sure what to do, but going home wasn't an option.

"I can't," was all he managed.

"He was a good kid," Big Joe replied. "What happened to him?"

Alex reached out to grab another beer.

"This was my fault," he replied. Alex tried to remain stoic, but his eyes watered and his face fell slightly. "He called me just the day before, asking about a helium tank. I even told him where to buy one."

Leslie appeared from across the room and moved around Big Joe delicately, putting her arm over Alex's shoulder. Her eyes were heavy and she spoke with concern, "Hey Alex."

"Hey."

"I'm so sorry about Will. I've been thinking about him all day. It fucking sucks."

"Hey! Watch your language," Big Joe smirked as he handed Leslie a beer.

"Whatever." She rolled her eyes. "There are no other words I could say. Swear words seem the most appropriate, don't you think, Alex?"

Alex stared into the crowd as Rachel walked through the front door. Alex rose abruptly and walked toward her.

"Rach?" he asked calmly.

"Hey Alex!"

"What are you doing here?" Alex asked with uncertainty.

Rachel squinted with a look of confusion.

"I was actually looking for Will. We were supposed to meet tonight and I've been trying to reach him all day, but I can't get ahold of him."

Alex's face sobered. He grabbed Rachel by the arm. "Can you come outside for a minute?"

Rachel was reluctant but Alex pulled on her, and she followed him to the front lawn. "What's going on, Alex? Why are you acting so weird? If Will doesn't want me here, it's fine! I'll just leave."

"No, no, it's not that." Alex shook his head and wiped his palms on his jeans. "I have some really bad news to tell you."

Rachel's eyes went soft and she looked at him with her full attention. Alex reached for her hand and held on to it. He cleared his throat.

"Will died last night."

A great silence grew between them as Rachel stared at Alex. She was quiet, her hand against her chest.

"He fucked up. He took a hit of some helium and apparently, that stuff could kill you. I had no idea, I mean, I've done it a hundred times but... Will died last night, because of it."

Rachel shook her head. Leslie opened the front door and saw the two of them talking on the lawn. She made her way to Rachel's side.

"What's going on?" she asked.

"Why didn't you tell me?" Rachel demanded, tears in her eyes as she looked at Leslie.

"I'm sorry Rachel. I thought you knew."

A sob escaped Rachel. "We were supposed to go to dinner. I saw him last night at the pet store. We made a date."

"I'm really sorry," Alex said. He wiped his eyes with the back of his hand. Other kids appeared on the lawn and watched their interaction; some classmates began to cry. "This really fucking sucks!" Alex yelled. "This was all my fault."

"Alex, please, what does that mean? I don't understand what happened."

Alex put his head in his hands and sank to the ground. Rachel knelt down in front of him and wrapped her arms around his neck in a hug.

He cried into her shoulder, "I told him where to buy it. I told him exactly what to do."

Rachel held on to him and let him cry, tears flowing down her face. "Don't do this to yourself. It wasn't your fault. Will loved you, Alex. He would never let you take the blame for this."

The reality of my death had settled in, the painful energy. I could feel it as I watched them suffer. Alex and Rachel held each other until they both stopped crying; finally they stood, vulnerable and in the comfort of each other's embrace.

"I'm sorry, I need to go now," Rachel whispered. She let go of Alex's hand and turned toward her car. She fumbled in her purse for her keys, tears blinding her vision. She finally unlocked her door and sat inside the vehicle. She took several deep breaths and forced her brain to absorb what Alex had just told her.

"Will is dead," she muttered.

She couldn't understand it.

Alex approached Leslie and watched with her as Rachel sat in her car for several more minutes, her head resting on her steering wheel. "Should we go to her?" Leslie asked sadly.

"She's in shock. I'll call her tomorrow and check on her."

Rachel's car started and she began to pull away from the curb.

Leslie closed her eyes as tears fell on her cheeks.

"Fucking sucks," she whispered.

Chapter
Twenty-Two

I fucked up. I didn't mean to kill myself. It was an accident.

After the initial shock of seeing my dead body, and watching my mother and father painfully struggle through that first night of turmoil, things started to happen to me, to my spirit. I was alone in the darkness, but I felt alive for the first time. I was pulled away from my family and I was left suspended in space, waiting.

Images of my life flashed before me. Every important moment—all the milestones, the love from my parents, the disappointments, and all the lessons that I needed to learn.

I had so many questions, and longed for complete understanding. I had an overwhelming feeling that it would all come to me, eventually. To be patient.

Then the movie ended, just like that. Lights out. Blackness again.

I had no sense of time anymore and I wasn't afraid of the dark; in fact, I had never felt more calm and relaxed. It was as if the veil over my life's purpose had been lifted. It was a mistake what had happened to me, but that was part of the lesson. I *hadn't* unlocked a very important box. I *hadn't* learned to accept myself or to love myself. I was in constant need of validation from my friends. I needed their attention—to feel popular, to feel love. It was hard for me to fight for myself, to put my own needs first, to go after what I wanted. I made excuses and leaned on the fact that my mother needed me, but deep down inside, I knew that I was afraid.

The gypsy had been right. My life had been in danger and I couldn't see it. I was blind to it.

As I gained more acceptance of what had happened to me, I started to glow. Soft at first, I noticed a speck of light illuminating in the darkness. I had no hands, feet, legs, or body. My presence felt insignificant in the vast darkness.

As I continued to illuminate the space around me, more spheres appeared in the darkness. Energies I recognized as my aura became brighter at our reunion. There was no fear, anger, or sadness and regret. I only felt love and understanding.

Then it happened: An energy emerged, and instantly I was taken back to a time I remembered, a time long ago. I was reunited with my soul brother.

"I've waited so long, to be with you again," he stated.

We moved forward through the space between us and fused into one sphere. It felt like home again.

"I have always been with you; I watched you meander through your life lessons like an amateur, but I am proud of you and I always loved you. I'm ready to teach you now, to show you better ways."

I stood in his aura as he wrapped me with a force. "There are so many memories being downloaded, this is unbelievable," I said. I caught glimpses of my many past lives.

My soul brother laughed. "We've been family a long time, Will. It's so good to have you home again. We have so much work to do, but I am here to help you gain the understandings that you have forgotten, to help you heal and give strength to your Earth family, who are now suffering. The things we do are important to the evolution of your spirit and will prepare you once again for your next soul reincarnation."

"How could I forget you?" It seemed impossible that I wouldn't remember my soul brother or all the experiences of my past lives, but they continued to present themselves. "How could I not remember this?" *This is incredible.*

"We've shared many lifetimes together. You don't remember because it's done this way on purpose. You're always given a clean slate when you reincarnate to help you move forward in life and in learning your lessons, without the angst of yearning to be back home. The lessons you are taught are so valuable; understanding all the boxes you left opened and unopened will help you in your next lifetime and elevate your soul for future insights."

Hope was important. Dreams were important. Love was important.

I realized that while in the darkness, I felt whole again.

My entire life, I'd been missing something, trying to fill a sadness that I couldn't quite put my finger on. I understood now that I came from a place that my memory forgot but my soul never did—that's why there was loneliness, a hole that I couldn't explain, but could feel.

"But there was always a loneliness," I questioned.

"Yes, there is. They are called voids. You tried to fill your voids looking for false friendships and attention from people who didn't matter. You tried to fill your loneliness with drugs and alcohol, an easy remedy to hide the pain and stress inside you."

I didn't realize I was trying to fill the voids, but my poor decisions confirmed that I was doing so, unconsciously.

"Voids can only be filled with love for yourself. Your soul comes from a place of unconditional love, and that is what you need to fill the void and loneliness. Had you loved yourself, you would never do drugs; you would never think less of yourself to put poisons in your body, or find yourself unworthy or needing of validation."

"Okay, I understand. Had I loved myself, I wouldn't have tried to please everyone around me; I would have done what was best for me and followed my hopes and dreams."

"Yes. To love yourself would have required you to view yourself with positive emotions. Emotions such as love and hope and courage instead of fear and doubt. It matters. It matters to the universe and it matters to your soul family, how you view yourself and how much love you give. It's all about positivity and higher thinking."

The feeling of the void was gone now. I felt incredible. I felt whole again. Complete. Loved.

"There's one more family member you need to meet." My soul brother stepped out of my aura. "Close your mind and just *feel*."

I did what I was told and I closed my thoughts. A slight tremor rippled my auric field and then a flood of what felt like pouring water all around me. I received visions of waterfalls and pools of natural springs with beautiful crystalized sand beneath my feet. I could feel the warmth of sunshine fill my soul as a breeze brushed across my face. I smelled lavender and sage, and then the memory of the gypsy lady popped into my head.

I opened my mind and there she was, the one I had been looking for, right in front of me.

"Hello William. We meet again."

She no longer held the appearance of the gypsy. She was an orb of light, like all the others.

"I am your guardian angel," she stated.

"You were there in person," I gasped. I was in awe of her power over me and desperate to get closer to her, to feel her love for me. "I thought you were a figment of my imagination."

She laughed. "I was there to help you, but only you could see me."

"I didn't listen to you. I didn't understand."

"Yes, I know. That's why you are here."

"Can I come closer?" I was propelled forward and we collided, her warmth like sunshine, washing away any pain and sorrow I still harbored, rinsing it away like water over sand.

"I hold you, your soul in my grasp. I offer you strength on the next part of your journey with your soul brother. I heal parts of you that you cannot heal on your own and I give you blessings of great faith as you embark on this next endeavor."

"Can you stay with me, can you come with us?" I asked. I didn't want her to leave; I wanted to hold on to her for as long as I could. "Thank you doesn't seem appropriate enough." I clung to her.

"You don't need to thank me, Will. I love you. I want the very best for you, and I leave you now in good hands with your brother. I promise you, we will see each other again, when it's time."

I stepped away from her and felt her beauty leave me.

She was gone, and as my new world began to illuminate, I watched a darkness overshadow my old world. The loss of my energy on Earth rippled through my family and classmates, knocking down the people who loved me, and who were now left to pick up the pieces.

Rachel drove on autopilot through the streets of our small town. I sat in the seat next to her. She took the appropriate turns and drove the appropriate speed, but was blank. She stared at the road in front of her, her face painfully concerned and her breath rapid in her chest. Her hands trembled as they gripped the steering wheel, her knuckles white.

I wanted to console her, to explain to her that this wasn't her fault. I was such a jerk anyway. *"You could do far better than me, Rach,"* I said to her, to someone who couldn't hear me. *"Don't waste your energy feeling sad about what had happened between us. It was a blessing. You were the only girl I ever had sex with."* I chuckled. *"Thank God I had sex before I died. Thank you Rachel!"* I leaned close to her. *"Can you hear me, Rach? Do you see me?"* I sat back in the passenger seat and smiled at my obnoxiousness. "No one can see you or hear you, dumbass."

Rachel pulled into her driveway and turned off the car. She leaned back on the headrest and her face crumbled. Her cell phone rang and rang, endless. She needed support around her, someone who understood what she was feeling. Alex and Leslie would have helped her, if she had let them.

The front door opened and Rachel's stepfather came out on the porch. He stood rigidly with his arms crossed and waited for Rachel to open the car door. He held a white piece of paper in his hand.

A few moments passed; eventually he walked down the stairs leading to the sidewalk and knocked on the driver's side window.

Rachel sprang up in her seat and wiped at her tears. She rolled her window down.

"I'm sorry sir, I didn't see you standing there."

"What the hell are you doing, sitting in your car?" He was angry.

"Oh, nothing, it's just that... Um, I had recently heard some horrible news regarding a friend of mine and...I'm sorry." Rachel's voice wavered and she struggled to hold back her emotions, but it wasn't working. She started to cry again as she vigorously wiped at her eyes. Her stepfather stood back from the window, recoiling at her show of emotions.

I could feel her fear. "He's a nobody, Rachel," I whispered. I could see all of who he was: a lonely man who hated himself deeply. His abusive ways were obvious even to Rachel, but she was afraid of him. As much as I could, I wrapped my arms around her and tried to give her the strength she needed to face him.

"So, what happened?" he asked, his eyes narrowed in on her face.

Rachel took a few deep breaths and calmed herself. "A friend of mine died," she whispered. Her hands remained gripped to the steering wheel.

Her stepfather's face changed: His lips pursed as his eyes scanned the interior of the vehicle. "Drugs?"

Rachel remained silent.

"Do you have any idea how many friends I have lost fighting for our military? Do you have any idea what *real* loss is?"

Rachel looked up at her stepfather. "I'm sorry?" she replied.

He handed her the white piece of paper. "Go to the grocery store and get these items. When you return I don't want to see another tear fall from your face, do you understand? I don't want you upsetting your mother."

Rachel took the sheet of paper and stared at it blankly. Her eyes were beginning to swell from rubbing them so fiercely. The mascara on her eyelashes created a darkened shadow just above her cheekbones. She silently rolled her window up and put her car in reverse. Her stepfather remained in the driveway as she drove down the street.

"What a son of a bitch!" I said to her. "Fucking dick, huh Rach?" I hated talking to myself, but hoped that I was reiterating the things she already knew.

I watched helplessly as Rachel fumbled for the radio. She turned on a station and a sad song came through the speakers. She continued to drive as more tears fell from her eyes.

"Oh God Rachel, it's really not that bad. This *music!*" I motioned to choke myself to death, squeezing my imaginary neck and sticking out my tongue at her. "Ugh." I rolled my eyes at myself.

I pressed the button to change the channel of the radio station. Rachel looked down with surprise as the music switched, rock and roll now exploding out of the speakers.

"Holy shit!" I yelled. "I actually turned the radio channel."

I looked at Rachel. She briefly stopped crying and reluctantly pressed the button to turn the channel back.

That same song was still playing. I could see her getting emotional again. "God, Rachel! This is so awful. Pick a better song, a cheerful song, something to rock out to."

I hit the button and the channel changed again. "YES!" I wanted to high five Rachel, but she couldn't grasp what was happening to her, and she couldn't see me anyway.

She stopped crying again and stared at the radio. "What the hell?" she asked herself. "I've got to get this radio checked."

Chapter

Twenty-Three

I continued to practice communicating more effectively. I wanted desperately to engage my family and to relay to them somehow that I was okay. I wanted to heal, and I wanted them to heal. I needed to get to the next spiritual level and reincarnate, and I could only do that by healing others.

Heaven was a beautiful place, it was home and I wished that my family could understand the process. The energy between the two dimensions was so different, the energy on Earth dark and the energy in Heaven light. I cared about my family and friends, so I waited and watched them, but I was always happy to get back home to Heaven, to the lightness and to the love. It wasn't long before I was spending less and less time on Earth and more time in Heaven, reacquainting myself with my soul family.

It was hard to describe who I was now. I was energy, a light that carried truth, understanding, and love. I could do anything I wanted. I could be human again, if I wanted to live another lifetime. I could visit Earth and see my family, if I wanted to. I could stay in Heaven and learn from my spirit guides or my guardian angel, if I so desired.

Or I could do nothing but exist in peace and harmony with my energy and with my soul family. Beauty was beyond beauty in Heaven, in a sense that I could feel beauty, not just see it. Love was beyond love—unconditional, accepting, peaceful love. There was no dark energy, no anger, no ego, no sickness, no worry or injustices.

It was magical.

But I continued to go back to Earth. It was necessary for me to witness the suffering caused by my actions and to help my family move forward through their mourning so that they could begin the process of healing.

No one needed more healing than my parents.

I had always gone to church when I was young. My father and I would sit in the pew, quietly listening to the priest go on and on and on. When I was old enough, I became an altar boy, helping the priests during mass and wearing that long robe that I hated.

Now, I watched as my father picked up the office phone and dialed the funeral parlor.

"Hello," a man answered.

"Hello, this is William Daring's father. I believe that Father Edward has contacted you regarding the services for my son."

"Oh, yes sir. We are very sorry for your loss. We have heard only good things regarding Will and we hope that our services can bring him the type of honor and respect that he deserves."

My father took a deep breath and closed his eyes. "Yes, thank you. So, Tuesday then?"

"Yes sir. Tuesday the calling hours will be from 4:00 to 8:00 and then mass and burial the following morning."

"Okay."

"Do you need us to do anything else for you, sir?"

My father rubbed his forehead. "No, that will be all. Thank you."

He hung up the phone and sat in a small chair next to the desk. Paperwork had piled up and several used coffee mugs were dispersed about the room. My father was a stoic man. He did the right things, worked hard, followed rules, and he had always been an emotionally conservative person. I had never seen him cry before.

His eyes crumbled and turned red; the pain and loss rippled through his face and made strange contortions of his features. Years of pent-up frustration and worry lived on the surface of his emotions, coming together with the grief of my passing. It was painful to watch him suffer. I wanted to tell him that this pain would be temporary. It wouldn't last forever, and there would be light and he would learn to live more present in his life. He would appreciate more deeply the things that he had.

But he cried and I circled him with my energy the best that I could.

***

I never liked funerals and I certainly didn't like my own. I watched the darkness of a storm cloud dim the lighting in the church as a low rumble of thunder rolled in the far distance.

My mother walked the aisle toward the front, her body thin and feeble. She steadied herself occasionally on a pew, resting to gain strength in order to continue forward. My father remained strong for appearances, but his hands shook. An occasional wave of grief would wrinkle through his chin. Rachel stood alone in the back, scared of what she might see or feel, her thumb raw as she massaged the clasp of her purse, tissues gripped so tightly that they fell into pieces toward the floor.

Alex gave a speech.

"He was my best friend," he started.

"And you were mine, Alex. I'm still here for you," I replied.

"Every day I miss him. I pick up my phone sometimes and dial his number, a habit that I can't seem to shake. I think sometimes that this is all a dream, a very bad dream that I can't seem to wake up from."

"I miss you too, Alex. I wish you understood more. I'll be watching you. I'm excited to see what you do now, how you will handle my death and how you will help others. I know that you can do this. You have a strength that no one else has."

"Moving forward seems impossible, but it's necessary. Will wouldn't want us to live in any other way but positive."

"Keep opening your boxes, Alex. I'll be rooting for you, all along the way."

Alex was a superstar to many people and had a positivity that was contagious. If Alex was silent long enough, he could hear my thoughts and encouragement. He had strong intuition and he trusted himself.

I could hear the emotions and concerns of my people, as if I were receiving multiple text messages—a constant ring of dinging, every second, every thought, every worry, and every feeling.

"Why did this happen?"

"Is this my fault?"

"How could I have helped him? I just spoke to him the day before it happened."

"I should have known he was in trouble."

"What will become of Linda?"

My family looked for an explanation as to why I had done this to myself and how they could have prevented my death. I could feel the doubt and the lack of faith and trust in what the universe had planned for me. But it was time to move on. It was time to heal from the trauma and to move forward with love in their hearts and for one another. It all started with Alex.

After the funeral, Alex and Rachel planned a vigil together in my honor. A soft glow of candles and cell phones lit up the town green, adjacent to our old high school. Counselors were on site to help anyone who needed the extra support. Rachel also incorporated a few women, energy healers, from her yoga studio.

The crowd of students sat on yoga mats and blankets, legs crossed and eyes closed. The aroma of sage and incense filled the air and an impressive fire burned as the woman led the prayer.

"Take this moment to breathe in and breathe out. Let your thoughts slip away. Concentrate on the present. You are always evolving, you are safe, you are accepted, and you are loved." The women meditated. They focused on my soul, sending positive affirmations as I crossed over into my new dimension.

"*Om Shanti Om.*" The healers drummed and rattled as they chanted softly.

"I am peace. We are peace," the crowd repeated.

"*Om Prema Om.*"

"I am love. We are love."

The healers placed their hands on students' shoulders as they prayed, "You are blessed. May you heal your pain with love and courage and let go of fear and confusion."

I thought it was awesome.

The meditation ceremony was an optimistic experience for Alex and Rachel and I could tell they felt proud, as if they contributed something to my life. Perhaps now they could accept my death, in however small a way, and start to move from their heartache. They shared a blanket at the vigil, sitting closely. Alex held Rachel's hand and occasionally their eyes would meet in an affectionate stare. They both shared the same traumatic emotions regarding my passing and they seemed to be helping one another.

I was surprised by Alex's attentiveness toward her. It was unlike him to be so selfless. I was proud of him. He was opening a box for himself by being loving and vulnerable, focusing on what he could do for Rachel and my family instead of pursuing what they could do for him. I could see that she responded to him positively too, the way she would check her makeup and lipstick when he wasn't looking.

I could feel the chemistry between them. It was strong and protective. They were beginning to trust one another—and for the first time ever, my best friend actually cared about someone sincerely.

Alex was growing.

Chapter

Twenty-Four

My mother paced the house nervously while Lola followed her around, whimpering for attention. My mom ignored her and put on her coat. She walked to the front door, her slippers slapping against the floor, then descended the porch to the sidewalk in front of our house. She looked both ways, up and down the street and stood waiting for several minutes.

Carol poked her head out of her entrance. "Mrs. Daring? What are you doing honey, do you need something?" She stepped out onto her front porch and wrapped her sweater around her body. Life had been quiet in my neighborhood since I died and Carol seemed genuinely concerned for my mother.

My mother tried to wave her off, but Carol persisted.

"Do you need me to call someone, Mrs. D? Your sister perhaps?"

Finally, my mother turned around and walked back up the stairs and into her house. She didn't look at Carol or say a word. She was concentrating on Alex. He promised he'd be there.

Alex was busy, distracted by his need to contact Rachel. He was worried about her and wanted to check on her. He had mentioned stopping by my mom's house but he didn't know that his words would penetrate my mother's mind with obsession; he didn't know that she would wait for him all day. As often as I talked about my mother with Alex, I never led on to how obsessive she was and how difficult she could be at times. I never talked about it.

My mother went back to the window. Lola barked at her and jumped on her leg, pulling at her sweater with her teeth. She continued to stare.

What would I have done for her, if I were alive? What if, instead, her sister had died? How would I have helped her cope with that? My aunt was helpful, but my mother needed to live with someone who could be with her sometimes. My aunt wasn't committed to that type of care. No one was. No one could possibly understand the extent of her needs the way I did, and I couldn't convey that now. The only other person who could possibly understand was my father, and he was suffering. He couldn't be asked to help assist her.

She was on her own.

It grew dark and Alex hadn't shown up. He wasn't coming.

"Mom, he's not coming."

My words were thoughts whirling around her head. She knew, too, that he wasn't coming.

She finally sat on the couch. She hadn't touched a bit of food all day. She didn't have her tea. She had Lola, who hadn't gone outside and whose food dish was empty. In fact, even my mother's refrigerator was pretty bare, and her bed hadn't been slept in. She paced the house at night and watched from the window as the sun rose in the east. Occasionally she stood in the hallway and stared into my room, still and frozen, confused as her eyes remained stoic and emotionless.

I tried to wrap her with my light. I swirled around her and begged her to snap out of it. I wasn't coming back. She had to figure this out on her own or she wouldn't survive.

Survival was never a priority for my mother. She didn't fear her own death; in fact, she never really wanted to live in the first place. It was easy to see, with my soul brother's guidance, how my mother's thoughts sabotaged her own healing and growth.

Once her mother died, death had become a curiosity, a channeled outlet for her to dream about, believing that her own reality was so bad, that death was a better option—or at least something that gave her hope.

What she couldn't see was that the struggle outward and upward would have healed her, saved her. She needed to fight for herself. Struggle was the lesson and no one on Earth was given a free pass. My mother's lessons continued to resurface; again and again they showed themselves in sickness, addiction, social confinement. These struggles offered her the opportunity to grow and fight to overcome the darkness, but she never overcame. There was no escape from the struggle, not in this lifetime or in the next.

Had my mother overcome the obstacles in her life, she would have felt positivity, pride, strength, and confidence. Her thoughts would have been refocused on success instead of failure, optimism and hope instead of sadness and poor health.

Her thoughts mattered. She needed to open so many boxes, one box at a time.

A few baskets of flowers from the funeral parlor littered the countertop along with a gift basket of wine, cheese, and crackers. She stared hard at the basket then walked to the counter to lift the bottle of wine from under the confetti and wrappings. Opening the drawers, she looked passionately for a bottle opener and, having found one, she fought to open the bottle. The cork eventually gave with a big pop, spilling red wine all over. My mother frantically poured herself a glass and drank it quickly. She grabbed a box of crackers and with the bottle under her arm, she walked to the couch.

The bottle didn't last long. Finally, she put her head down on the couch pillow and stretched her legs out.

Her day was over. I could feel her energy let it go as she drifted off to sleep, hopeful that perhaps she would see Alex again tomorrow, hopeful that this misery would subside and that perhaps, somehow, I would be with her again soon.

"I am with you, Mom."

I wished her mind to have a restful sleep. *"Tomorrow is a new day,"* I whispered as I fluttered my energy around her face and lips.

"Goodnight, Mom."

Chapter

Twenty-Five

As the clock chimed midnight, a clinking sound came from my mother's basement.

At first I thought it was her furnace and I cursed myself for not having a new one installed before I died. My mother was asleep and I was enjoying watching Lola resting on the sofa.

The noise was getting louder—like someone was moving furniture, the obnoxious scraping of metal chairs on a concrete floor. Lola picked her head up and growled lightly. She sensed it too.

The puppy woke up, stretching her legs leisurely, she sauntered toward the basement doorway. She sniffed around the edges and then barked timidly, as if not sure if she should stay and investigate or run and hide.

I was curious.

I went through the door. I could hear voices and smell smoke, as if someone had just lit a cigarette. My aura was strong, and I knew that whatever or whomever I was going to encounter, I could handle.

It had never crossed my mind when I was alive, but now that I had passed on, I knew without a doubt: I didn't walk this earth alone. Other spirits remained here as well.

"Your mother's home is filled with a negative energy and it is thick. Can you feel it?"

If I had a heart, I would have clung to it. My soul brother surprised me at times, appearing out of nowhere.

"Can we put bells on you?" I asked. "Maybe a warning signal, some kind of system to let me know when you'll be dropping out of the sky."

His light blinked as if he were proud of his skill set, but then he continued to speak, his tone solemn. "These unwelcomed entities need to be dealt with. It would make my job easier if I could put bells on them, but that's not how it works."

"What are they?" I asked.

"They are the walking dead," he replied. "This is an important lesson, Will: to understand the walking dead and negative energy. If your mother has any chance of healing herself and if you have any chance of reincarnating, they need to go."

"What does that mean, if my mother has any chance?"

"These entities can attach themselves to human spirits, causing chaos and unbalance between the living and the dead, creating symptoms such as mental illness, depression, and even more severe problems."

In the basement, five chairs circled a round table for playing cards. Rugged men came and went, walking through the basement walls as if material items such as concrete or brick and mortar didn't even exist. Some sat and drank whiskey; others lingered in the dark corners of the cellar, watching and waiting for their turn to play. One spirit had half a face, his jawbone exposed and shaking violently as he laughed at another spirit's lack of hair, his head scalped and parts of his skull missing around the crown.

The dead kept coming, their injuries exposed and their clothing disheveled and dirty as if they just climbed out of their gravesites specifically to roam the earth at the midnight hour.

"My mother's house is old and slightly run down, but it's not this old," I mentioned. "Why are all these spirits here?" The house wasn't old enough to be home to this many people.

"In another lifetime, the place where we stand was entirely something else, a battleground and an old tavern where these men congregated and socialized."

I watched silently.

"The walking dead continue to exist among the living, stuck in their Earth minds, clinging to the memories of their human bodies and refusing to move forward in their evolution."

Some approached me, trying to navigate what it was they felt or recognized. They recognized the bright light in me, a new soul who recently passed over from the world of the living to that of the dead. It was something they chased every time they roamed the earth, to no avail.

"They are real and they are everywhere, stuck in this dimension," he stated.

I thought about how often I felt depressed and negative, how some days I just didn't feel good or feel quite like myself. I wondered how often the walking dead were with me, coming through my bedroom and playing cards in my basement.

"They wait in the darkest corners of our world, standing on street sidewalks and walking through buildings and homes. They follow the sick, cling to the addicted, and seek after those who live egotistical lives, chasing material items and artificial human experiences."

"Why don't they evolve?" I asked.

"They are lost souls, victims to the negative forces that keep them in between dimensions. Some don't believe in the light, and are often frightened and unaware that they are even dead. Some never learned to open their boxes and no one is here to pray for them, to help them cross over."

I was beginning to understand.

"Negativity attracts negativity, Will, both from the living and the dead." He paused. "Staying among your Earth family comes with the understanding that it is supposed to be temporary and not without risk or warning."

"I feel confident that I will not fall into the space of the walking dead," I said. "My mother's house is like a magnet, her being sickly and depressed. My mother has been easily susceptible."

"That's exactly right, but we can help her. We can clear this space and ban the energies. I have faith that you can do this yourself."

I took a moment and then prayers began to fill my thoughts.

I stepped away from my soul brother and quickly circled the room, creating a tornado of energy and a whistle so piercing that dogs began to bark throughout the neighborhood. My prayers were strong. "I banish all energies that are less than love, with the light of my grace. Be gone forever, for you have no power here. I release you and send you on your way."

One by one the spirits disappeared, leaving only the stench of smoke and the echo of laughter. "These spirits are gone now, but they can easily return if your mother doesn't make changes to her energy. Energy attracts energy."

This was going to be a difficult task. My energy was exhausted. It had been two months since I died and my soul brother thought it necessary to bring me back to Heaven, for spirit revitalization. My new opportunities were boundless as I was paired up with other souls of similar ages and similar experiences to gain more insights and understandings. Thoughts were shared telepathically, for we had no shape or form.

My soul brother was beautiful. I called him brother because of his masculine energy, but we were neither male nor female beings. Gender was a human experience and had nothing to do with spirit or soul. In fact, a soul could live several lives, both male or female, or some other type gender. It didn't matter; it was the same soul.

We had different soul lives, too. My soul brother's spiritual age was one hundred lifetimes older than mine, which made the essence of light around his aura radiate with not just bright light, but color too: purple softness with hues of blues and yellows that radiated around him. He was beautiful to see, and powerful to feel. I was home again.

His joy could be felt through vibration. When he approached me, the energy around my orb trembled, as if a five-point earthquake were shaking the universe, his energy was so powerful and intoxicating. His purpose was to guide me through my new world, to reteach me many of my forgotten skills and to reconnect me with the past of my many lives, so my insights could be combined and used to elevate my frequency.

It seemed a heavy task but an important one.

I was determined to succeed.

Chapter

Twenty-Six

Rachel's semester break was over and she was finally returning to school in Boston. Alex was on his way to say goodbye to her when he decided to stop by my mom's house to check on her.

He parked his car in the usual spot. The garbage can was overflowing. My mother wasn't doing much for herself. She had attempted to mow the lawn, but was not strong enough to pull the cord to start the lawnmower. I had done everything for her. She even got lost in the grocery store and struggled with putting gas in the car, a task she hadn't done in over a decade.

Alex stepped up to the porch that he had climbed so many times before. He stood at the door and rang the bell, waiting for my mother to answer. A few minutes passed before Alex knocked hard on the glass window, careful not to break it. Still, no one came to the door.

Through the glass, he could see Lola dancing around and whining, right in front of the living room entrance.

Alex checked the doorknob. It was unlocked. "Mrs. D? Hello? Anyone home?"

Lola jumped on his leg, begging to be picked up.

"Hey puppy. Boy, you are getting big."

The living room and kitchen were empty. "Mrs. D? Are you here?"

He looked down at Lola. "Maybe she's with her sister, huh Lola?"

The house was disorganized but it looked like Lola had been fed.

"Come on girl, let's get you outside. I'm sure you need to go to the bathroom." Alex stood on the front porch and watched Lola squat down in the neighbor's yard. He chuckled under his breath. "Good job, Lola."

"Alex," he heard softly behind him.

"Mrs. D!" he exclaimed. He looked her over. She was wearing pajamas and her hair was sticking up in all directions. "Where were you? I was calling your name. I hope you don't mind but I let Lola out."

My mom looked at him oddly, then turned around and walked into the house.

Alex whistled, "Come on Lola, let's go!"

Lola paused to smell the earth beneath her feet, then ran gallantly up onto the front porch. Alex followed her, then stood at the entranceway into the living room and waited to be invited in. My mom continued to her bedroom.

Alex stood there waiting and eventually wandered into the house and leaned into the doorway of my mother's bedroom. He knocked softly. "Mrs. D, before I leave, do you need me to do anything for you?"

"No!" she yelled, her voice dark and husky. "Just go away."

Alex pushed open the door. Her bedroom was gloomy and the window blinds were pulled down. Several wine bottles cluttered the nightstand and her clothes were thrown all over the floor. Alex adjusted the blinds to let the sunlight in.

"Mrs. D, you can't stay in bed all day." He sat next to her. "What can I do for you, while I'm here?"

My mom stuffed her face into her pillow. Alex placed his hand on her back and encouraged her to talk to him. He knew her well enough that if he paid her some attention, she would usually come around.

She started to cry. "I can't stop thinking about him," she muttered. "I don't want to live anymore."

Alex reached for a tissue box and handed her some Kleenex. "I know it's been hard on you, but Will wouldn't want to see you like this, suffering. He would want you to move forward and start living again. Maybe you need to speak to someone who understands, a therapist maybe."

She needs a healer, a shaman perhaps, I thought.

My mother sat up, putting her feet on the ground. Her face was still and her eyes were red from crying. "Those people can't help me," she said angrily.

Alex sighed. "Have you eaten today? Would you like me to make you something?"

Silence.

Alex walked into the kitchen, turned on the teakettle, and opened the refrigerator. He prepared a small plate of cheese and crackers and placed it on the counter. He opened the cabinet beneath the sink looking for garbage bags. Three empty bottles of wine were hidden underneath. He pulled them out and put them on the counter.

"Look in the closet," I said.

His instincts were good. Alex went to the hallway closet and opened the door. Inside were two large garbage bags full of empty wine bottles.

I never talked much about my mother's drinking with Alex. I was sure that this was a surprise to him.

"Check the bathroom cabinet," I whispered into the silence.

Alex started to roam the house, opening doors and other random closets, discovering more evidence hidden beneath items of necessities, of my mother's long-term problem.

My mom walked through her house and stood by the window overlooking the neighbors' yard. Alex followed her.

"Can I talk to you?" he asked.

She remained silent. Lola sat by her feet and put her head down on the floor.

I could see tears fall down her face, but she didn't look at Alex and she wouldn't speak.

"What's with all the empty wine bottles? They're stashed everywhere. Are you drinking, Mrs. D?"

The teakettle screamed, but Alex didn't move. He waited a few seconds to see if she would respond to him. She didn't. He reached out and held on to her arm and tried to turn her gently toward him. My mother's face shifted, and I was fearful for Alex. He didn't know entirely what he was dealing with.

"Take your hands off of me!"

"I'm not trying to hurt you, but I want to know what's going on with you. Will would not appreciate this if I left you here alone, drinking yourself through this depression and self-medicating with God knows what else."

Alex had known my mother since we were eight years old. He took liberties with her because he's seen her in some very vulnerable states of mind. Like the time we came home one night and she was passed out on the couch, halfway on the cushion and halfway on the cold floor. He'd helped me carry her to bed. I explained to him that sometimes the sleeping pills did a number on her, but I knew that she was drunk.

I could tell Alex felt weird to be in my house. It felt dark and lifeless, as if someone had pulled the plug on all the lights and the electricity had been shut off. Alex moved toward the kitchen and picked up the phone to dial 911.

"What are you doing?" my mother screamed.

"I'm getting you help. You're not staying here alone like this anymore. You need to talk to someone about what's happening with you, or you're just going to kill yourself."

"Please, Alex, don't." My mother tugged on his arm while he held the phone up to his ear.

"I promise to be good. I won't drink anymore. I'll talk to a counselor." My mother started to pace the kitchen floor.

"It's for the best, Linda."

"No Alex, it's not. I'd be better off dead than to go to the hospital again."

My mother lunged to grab the phone out of Alex's hand, wrestling with it, but he held her away while she swung at his chest. Patiently he restrained her as the phone continued to ring.

My mother started to cry and fell to the floor, sitting down with her face between her legs. Lola came to her and licked her hands, nudging her to respond.

The EMTs came in shortly afterward and placed my mother on a stretcher. Alex had also called my aunt, who rode with my mother to the hospital.

Alone in my kitchen, Alex slumped against the fridge, his strength drained. As I watched him struggle, I could see into his mind: He could picture me walking through the house, a big smile on my face, the excitement in my body language and eyes as I talked. But it was just a memory, a vision of an old me who had gone and vanished, like magic. Life had been turned upside down and everything that was true and real had changed.

He opened the door and looked back at Lola. "Come on girl," he said. "You need to come with me."

The emptiness was tangible; the house and all its contents seemed dead now that I was gone.

It didn't take long for my mother's health to fail after that. She had struggled mentally for years, and I knew that she would not tend well to my passing. Her vibe was low and her thoughts negative.

She didn't want to live anymore, not without me.

Chapter

Twenty-Seven

Alex drove silently across town toward Rachel's house. He thought fondly of my mother; I could tell that it really bothered him to see her so depressed.

He stopped at the jewelry store on his way. "I'm looking for something special, a going away gift," he said to the jeweler. "Something my friend could have and wear, a gift that could be a reminder of our friendship." The jeweler looked at Alex and nodded, a slight smirk on his lips.

He returned with several new pieces in his hand. "Take a look at these. They are simple yet practical, yet elegant. They don't scream, 'I love you,' but they speak very loudly, 'I like you very much.'"

Alex beamed and pointed at one. "This one is perfect!"

Alex cared about Rachel—it wasn't hard to tell. My death had left him feeling so vulnerable, so lost and hurt, and I think Rachel was the only one who could fill that space in his heart.

The parking lot was crowded as he returned to his vehicle; he looked deep in thought. The turmoil with my mother didn't sit well and saying goodbye to Rachel was going to be difficult.

Rachel's house was located on a quiet street lined with big oak trees and vibrant green front lawns. Her stepfather was there, packing her car. Alex approached him and introduced himself.

"Hello sir." Alex offered his hand in an effort to shake his. "My name is Alex."

Ray stared at him for a second then turned his back and continued to pack her car.

Alex lowered his hand and cleared his throat.

"He's a dick, Alex," I said. I knew he couldn't hear me, but I hoped he could feel my sentiment.

"Is Rachel home, sir?" Alex tried again.

Rachel's stepfather let out a big sigh of irritation.

"He's a miserable bastard, Alex. Don't even waste your time. Just walk past him and go to the front door." It was all I could do.

Alex politely waited and then moved to walk past him.

"Where are you going?" Ray said, abruptly.

Alex stopped and turned around. "I was going to knock on the front door."

"You can *stay* here and *wait* until she comes out." He said this lowly, almost as if in a growl.

Alex seemed surprised by his attitude but did what he was told.

The trunk hatch suddenly fell down on Rachel's stepfather's head, hitting him hard and causing him to lose balance. I couldn't help myself.

Alex grinned. "Are you okay, sir?"

"Son of a bitch, this goddamn car!" A small patch of blood appeared on his forehead, prompting him to wipe it with his sleeve. He glared at Alex then moved abruptly toward the house. "Rachel! You have a visitor!"

"He deserved it," I said. I watched as Rachel came out of her house. She looked beautiful, the way she moved down her front steps eager to see Alex, her energy full of excitement. I was grateful for the time she gave me. I didn't appreciate her enough while I was alive and wished I had tried harder. She was worth it.

As Alex watched her too, I could tell he was nervous. He wiped his hands on the front of his pants and stood awkwardly on the side of the driveway.

"Hey Alex! I'm so sorry, I didn't realize you were here."

"No, it's okay. I wasn't here long." Alex smiled. "I see you're all packed up and ready to go."

Rachel's cheeks flushed red and she twisted her hair around her fingers nervously. "Yeah, I'm leaving shortly." She leaned up against the stonewall that separated the yard from the driveway, resting slightly on Alex's shoulder. "I don't have much time here, my stepfather and all." Rachel nodded toward the house. "But I wanted to thank you." Their fingers touched slightly and they intertwined their hands. "You've been an incredible friend these past few months. I don't know how I would have survived without you."

Alex smiled deeply. "I was hoping we had more time together. Saying goodbye feels difficult."

Rachel looked at the ground. "Yeah, I know what you mean."

"Life has been really hard, and I learned after Will died that life is really short too. It's important to live fully and to value the things that we have. I really appreciate you, Rachel. This friendship between us has become a blessing to me, in so many ways. I look forward to our time together and as difficult as our distance may be, I hope we can still see each other." He pulled out the jewelry box from his back pocket. "I got this for you. It's nothing big or anything. I saw it and it reminded me of you. I wanted you to have it, to say thank you for being available to me, for being such a good friend."

She took the small package and opened it. The brightness of her eyes watered as she lifted the cross out of the box.

"Oh Alex, this is beautiful," she exclaimed. The necklace landed perfectly along her chest as Alex fumbled with the clasp. She lifted her hair off her neck and he fastened the necklace tight, securing it in place. The cross floated delicately above her breast line, perfect. She placed her hand on top of it and stared at Alex. They both stood quietly.

The front door opened suddenly, the screen hitting the side rail so loud that they both jumped at the unexpected interruption. Rachel's stepfather was approaching. She stood tall and kissed Alex on his lips. "I'm never taking this off," she whispered, then turned and was gone.

Ray stood near her car, his arms crossed, staring at Alex, expecting him to scram—quickly.

"Have a safe trip, Rach. Call me when you arrive," Alex yelled.

Rachel glanced back at him as she touched her necklace, then walked into her house.

Alex started to leave the driveway. "Goodbye sir," he said politely. The stepfather said nothing.

Alex smiled to himself. "Dick," he muttered under his breath. He started to laugh.

He suddenly appeared very happy.

It's what I would call *love energy*, and he had it beaming all around him.

Chapter

Twenty-Eight

Love energy was what propelled me back to Heaven, away from the depths of my mother's darkness and into the vastness of understanding that propelled me forward in my journey. I welcomed the break that my soul family offered me. My spirit soured whenever I was being "called back" and I radiated with this amazing light as I anticipated what might be to come.

More souls arrived at the gate as they welcomed me. The spherical glow of spirits lined perfectly in formation, guiding a pathway that I was to enter. One by one the spirits lit up, one sphere brighter than the other, like dominoes of light showing me the way. I moved along in awe at the energy, like bolts of lightning in its purest form of love and affection for me. I could feel the heat radiating and I trusted the path on which I moved. My spirit guides followed behind me as I passed them, encouraging me toward my destination.

I heard laughter and turned around.

"I could hear your thoughts." He chuckled. My soul brother swirled around me, playfully.

"It's amazing here," I said. "I'm always in awe at what I see and feel."

"Let's talk about this love energy. You are witnessing it with Alex and Rachel. How does it feel to you?"

"I recognize it. I felt the love energy for Rachel too."

"Yes, you did. You had tremendous love energy for her, even when you were young. You two are part of the same soul family, do you realize that? When she dies, you will be with her again. When you reunite, the two of you will share the memories of your past."

Everything made sense. "I was always connected to her; we were drawn toward each other in so many ways."

"That's right. As a human, you are born into a biological family on Earth but you also have a soul family, who is sent to you to teach you things about yourself and to learn from one another. They are sent to you in forms of friends, lovers, coworkers, classmates, and even pets and animals. You and Rachel taught each other many things. Mostly, you were learning how to overcome your shyness and self-doubt. You were brave in your pursuit of her. For Rachel, for the first time in her life she felt love and genuine affection from a male figure. That love energy is in her now and she can recognize it, although she still needs to overcome some of the trauma her stepfather has instilled in her. Alex will help her with that, and she will also teach him things about himself."

I was amazed that Alex had so much love energy for her. He had always needed attention from multiple sources, so I was surprised at his commitment toward her.

"Alex has also learned since you died, to give of himself without expectation from others," my brother said, knowing my thoughts. "He has learned to put other's needs first before his own. Alex is an older soul and the lessons come easy to him. He has a maturity that Rachel does not."

"Alex is definitely my soul family," I stated.

My brother laughed. "Absolutely he is."

My thoughts shifted. Alex seemed to always have it together. Me, on the other hand…I had squandered my life. I could have become so much more if I believed in myself.

"I held so many negative thoughts about who I was, foolish thoughts that weren't even warranted," I said. "Thoughts about how I looked, and whether I was cool or likable enough to even maintain friendships. The negativity was always in me. I don't know how I could have changed that."

"You were programmed that way by your life experiences, by your situation with your mother and how you were raised. These are all part of the journey to finding your way toward living for your highest good, living a soulful life without ego. For example, your aunt and your father and even Alex had talked with you about getting help for your mother and not letting it take over your life. You refused this help that was offered to you."

My soul brother's words stung a little, but he was right. It was possible that had I accepted help from my family, perhaps my mother would be in a better place mentally, and I would still be alive. Maybe that box would have led to many other different, more positive opportunities for the both of us.

"It was my ego that prevented me from accepting help. I didn't think anyone could care for her as well as I did, and I didn't want to be forced to live a life that I was unsure of. I was afraid."

241

"Your thoughts matter. It's like training for a marathon: You need to practice at positivity every day. Eventually, it becomes a part of you and you begin to see the blessings along the way."

"I was afraid to live," I said, speaking the words as they came to me. "Even college scared me, I made safe decisions for myself on behalf of my mother, but also, I didn't think I was worthy enough or smart enough to succeed."

"The truth is people did like you and even if they didn't, you still needed to love yourself as a person. You wasted so much time being *down* when you could have been *up*, hoping and dreaming and living life with excitement and energy. Alex had that about him—even amid the drama with his mother's sexuality, he was able to stay positive and work through the changes his family went through. You were always envious of Alex, but you carried the light within you too. *Everyone* carries the light. It's a matter of awareness."

I sighed, unconvinced. "I squandered my life in a pool of negativity and it was a wasteful place to be. I wish I knew better."

He started to move down the pathway and I followed him.

I was ready to ask for forgiveness. I understood life now, and I wanted a second chance. I wanted to live again, with hope that I would check different boxes, have different positive experiences and elevate my journey on Earth to the best it could be, with love for myself.

My soul brother shined down on me. "You could have become anything that you wanted to be. That's the whole point. Your dreams were endless, my boy."

My life could have been much more powerful and fulfilling, had I remained true to myself and loved myself above all else.

"You know what you have to do, right?" he asked.

"Yes. I need to forgive myself."

"This is all in the past now. You and I, we're moving forward. When you are ready, you'll get your second chance."

I closed my eyes and I forgave myself. It was my loss that was so significant, but it was my awakening that was going to propel me forward.

I forgave myself and I let it go.

Chapter
Twenty-Nine

Alex waited in his living room for almost an hour for Rachel to return his call. I knew he couldn't stop thinking about her. He wanted to see her again, to make sure that she was settled in school, that she was okay with her classes, and that she was moving on from my passing. He sat on his couch and fell back against the cushions. I watched him with amusement. Alex had a chance to evolve in a way that I couldn't. It was the one last thing I wanted to do for myself, watch Alex succeed.

"Why did I get so attached to her?"

Alex worked hard for his father's business. After high school he continued to immerse himself in learning the trade his father had taught him, ever since he was a little boy. His mother married Angie and just as quickly as life became unsettled, it settled—mostly because Alex was able to accept the things that were no longer in his control. He was motivated by love instead of fear and because of it, his life fell into place for him. Even though he may have felt uneasy and uncomfortable with the emotions he was feeling, I could see clearly what was happening and where he was heading. He needed to keep moving forward.

Leaning against the wall, his mother stood, her eyes focused on his face. Smirking, she said, "I would give everything I have to know what you are thinking right now."

Alex loved his mother and had a great deal of respect for the things that she went through, she *and* her wife.

"It's just Rachel," Alex said. "Can I ask you something, Mom?"

Alex's mom moved across the room faster than Alex could finish his sentence. "Of course honey. Ask me anything."

Vulnerability was not a familiar emotion for Alex, and although it made him feel awkward, it also made him feel alive. "Do you think I should tell her?" His eyes danced with the possibility as he stared at his mother. "Do you think I should tell Rachel how I feel about her? I mean, I think she sort of knows how I feel. I think she likes me too. It's just so hard with her being away and...I don't know. Maybe it was Will's death that connected us, but all I know is that I can't stop thinking about her. It drives me insane."

The energy Alex felt was so strong that he fidgeted unconsciously. He moved around the room, picking up picture frames and staring at them, inspecting the pillows and looking blankly at a magazine, then tossing it back onto the coffee table.

Alex's mom's face appeared soft and loving. She closed her eyes and inhaled a deep breath of pride. "I see," she stated. "Are you nervous about how you feel, or are you just afraid to tell her?"

"Mom, I'm not nervous to tell her...more like I'm nervous and afraid to feel these things. Sometimes I wish I could go back to the old me, dating girls and not caring at all about life or *feelings*. But I can't. It feels phony to me now; those girls hold no interest for me anymore. I can't even go to a party and enjoy myself; it's so boring and unproductive. I don't know what is happening to me."

With elegance, Alex's mom crossed one leg over the other and placed her hands together in her lap. "This is not the worst thing, Alex. You have to realize that you are getting older now and growing to be a more responsible young man. You lost your best friend in a tragic accident, and that sort of thing changes you. Life is short and precious. It isn't about partying and being reckless with women's hearts. It's not who you are anymore and I couldn't be more proud of that fact."

Alex was stilled by his mother's words. "It's weird, Mom, but after Will died, I felt an obligation come over me. It's real hard to explain, but it felt *good* to help people. Rachel helped me too but it was almost like… It was almost like it was meant to be. I felt right about what I was doing and the time we spent together. Does that make sense?"

"Absolute sense."

"And now, I think differently. Will died so suddenly. I could die just the same in some silly accident or crossing the street or even on a work site."

Alex's mom nodded, agreeing.

"I want to experience love and be excited and scared and understand all these uncomfortable feelings. I want to tell her how I feel and date her and kiss her face. I want to start to live again, but live in a way that feels real to me."

Standing up from the couch, Alex's mom beamed. "Oh Alex, that is so beautiful." She wrapped her arms around his body. "You get it, Alex. You completely get it."

Alex let his mother embrace him and seemed comforted by her unconditional love. "I love you, Mom. If anyone has taught me how to live a life without fear, it's you."

Alex's mom looked up at him, who was much taller than she. "Yes! But look how long it took me to *get it*! You're young and you understand so much more than I did at your age. You won't live in silence and deny yourself the things that you feel. I'm so proud of you!"

They held on to each other for a long moment. Alex lifted his head slightly. "So, do you think I should tell her?" He laughed.

Alex's mom laughed too. "Yes, you fool. I think you should tell her!"

Chapter

Thirty

It was the first time Alex drove to Boston. The ride seemed easy enough. He parked his car in the hotel garage and went to the front desk. The hotel was pleasant and suitable for his needs, bright and welcoming. After checking in, he made his way toward the bed and plopped his duffle bag onto the floor. Alex moved toward the windows and threw open the drapes to let the sunlight in.

"Wow," he stated as he looked out over Fenway Park. Memories of baseball games came flooding back, and I thought about how much we loved going to Fenway as kids. Alex stood at the window for ten minutes, watching the crowds of people walk over the bridge, toward the ball field. Vendors lined the streets selling game paraphernalia, baseball hats, T-shirts, and the classic sponge hands. It was as if I could smell the hot dogs and cotton candy from his hotel room.

Alex picked up his cell phone and dialed Rachel's phone number. I thought it was risky to surprise her with this unannounced visit but he'd opened a box and I wanted to see where it would lead him. I wanted to help him along the way, if I could, with my energy. It was easy with Alex; he was naturally positive.

Alex and Rachel had been talking regularly on the phone; texting and checking in with each other. It felt important that he see her in person; he was going to talk to her and tell her how he was feeling about their friendship.

The phone rang several times with no answer. He hung up and took a quick shower before heading to Boston College. The sun was setting; a pink sky stretched over the city. Alex smiled deeply as he dried himself off with a towel. Love energy had surrounded his aura and he was radiant.

He walked out into the streets; the air was full of noise and food smells and wonderful lights. The subway system, also known as the T, was a half block from his hotel.

Many empty seats were available on the train but Alex chose to stand. He wrapped his fingers around a bar for balance and the train began a subtle movement down the tracks. Around him, several people and some students, young with backpacks and eyes of determination, sat staring at their cell phones. I could feel Alex's energy as an anxious roll of nerves swirled around his belly like a nest full of honeybees.

The train stopped and the doors flew open, passengers eager to disembark onto the platform and into the streets. The walk toward the school was a quick one as he came upon the big sign that stated, *Welcome to Boston College.* He was in the right place.

Alex picked up his phone and dialed Rachel's number again.

"Hello," she answered.

"Hey, it's me."

"Hey!" she responded. "Sorry I missed your call earlier. I was stuck in class and we can't use our cell phones. What's up?"

He grinned. "I was just wondering what your plans were tonight?" He paused near the administration building: large, detailed with massive stonework all around the windows and along the entrance doorways. Alex walked up the steps, then turned and sat facing out onto the campus and watched the view of the sun setting.

"I was meeting up with a couple of friends for dinner, but nothing too exciting. How about you? What's going on back home?"

Alex looked down on the stair his foot rested on and kicked a few pebbles off to the side.

Ignoring her question, he asked, "So where are you now?"

"Um, I'm just sitting on my bed. I'm beat. I had two exams today and spent last night studying in the campus library."

"Yeah, that sucks."

"It's okay. They're over now. I feel relieved."

"That's great. You should be. I'm sure you'll pass them with flying colors." Alex paused. "I have to tell you, Boston College is unbelievably beautiful."

"Yes, it is. I feel very fortunate to attend school here."

"You're really lucky, Rachel. I mean, the church, the buildings, the green, the facilities…it's breathtaking. It feels safe too. It's comforting for me to know that you're in a safe and beautiful place."

Rachel started to giggle. "It sounds like you've been here before. Have you been doing some research on Boston College? I can promise you, the pictures won't do it any justice."

Alex laughed. "Yeah, something like that."

Rachel sighed. "I would give anything to have you come for a visit. It would do my soul some good to see your face again. I think about you so often and I wear your necklace every day. I place my hand over the cross and I pray for strength sometimes. I pray for you."

I watched Alex close his eyes and felt a strong emotion lodge itself in the middle of his chest. Her words were soft and sincere. Everything she said, he felt the same.

"So, anyway, I'm just sitting here, along this magnificent staircase, overlooking this beautiful green adorned with trees and benches, watching people walk by. This unbelievable church is in the distance."

It was 6:00. The steeple bells began to ring. The strike of a clock tower that rang through campus on the hour, every hour, the beautiful sound echoing through the space, through the phone and connecting Rachel and Alex in the exact moment.

"Alex? Are those church bells I hear?"

"Yes, I believe so."

"Well, that's so odd. I can hear them through your phone and I can also hear them on my campus." Rachel laughed. "What are the chances?"

Alex grinned. "I don't think it's a coincidence, Rachel."

Rachel paused. "What are you saying?"

"I'm saying that if you walk out of your dorm room and head to the church on your campus, it's possible you might find me standing there, waiting for you."

"*What*?! Wait a minute. You're here?!"

"Yes, I'm here." Alex couldn't suppress a laugh.

"Oh my god!"

The phone went silent.

"Rachel? Rach? Hello?" Alex looked at his phone, confused. "She hung up on me!"

"You freaked her out but she's probably on her way," I stated, laughing.

Straightening himself, he began to walk toward the church. I followed him.

I could feel Alex's sense of urgency as he walked toward the church in the distance. He started to run, looking at every person he passed. Looking for her.

As he finally neared his destination, he stopped to catch his breath. Moisture beaded on his hands and his face hurt from smiling.

Like a ghost out of nowhere, she came. She stood quietly and her chin dropped to her chest as she covered her eyes to wipe away the tears that were falling.

Alex went to her and lifted her chin with his fingers. "Please don't cry."

"I can't believe you're here," she managed through her tears. "I missed you so much."

Alex planted small kisses all along her face and cheeks and forehead. He pulled her tightly into his arms and held her for as long as she let him.

She was his home, and I knew it then: He loved her. He rocked with her in his arms, back and forth until she could speak again. She stared at him for a long moment and then he bent down and softly kissed her lips.

"Life is short, Alex," I said. *"Tell her that you love her."*

He grabbed her hand and they began to walk together, throughout the campus, both of them smiling, their eyes sparkling and their love energy strong. She talked amiably about her school and he listened, just happy to hold her hand and be with her, side by side.

Chapter

Thirty-One

I was being pulled away from Alex and Rachel.

It was my mother. She was giving up hope and I was being sent on one last-ditch effort to try to sway her spirit toward the light.

I struggled to bring myself to complete this impossible task, where my attempts seemed immature and inexperienced. My soul brother encouraged me to remain in a positive light and informed me that my energy frequency needed to remain elevated during my visit, which was to be very brief. I understood his message, which lifted me to a place of optimism.

I circled my mother's aura every step she took, like a hurricane of soft light that moved in circles up and down her body.

My mother had acknowledged to the doctors and to my aunt that she should not stay alone. When she returned from the hospital, my aunt moved in with her, yet as helpful as she tried to be, it was still very difficult. Aunt Bev was a strong, rigid woman—never married, no children. She didn't understand my mother, like I did, but she did her best to help her. She tried to challenge her in hopes that she would become more independent and self-sufficient. Her concern was genuine but what my mother needed was simple coping methods to help deal with her grief. She didn't need to be thrown into a fire pit of personal responsibility and obligation.

My mother was broken-hearted. As I followed her like a shadow, planting small kisses on her forehead and energy all around her body, she looked to her left side frequently, as if there were someone there, and I knew she could feel my presence.

My aunt cleaned the kitchen often, muttering under her breath how dirty the counters were and how disgusting the microwave was.

"Honestly Linda. You're home all day long. Do you think it's possible you could put some effort in picking up a little, taking the time to wipe down some counters and caring for your home?" Aunt Bev was never one to mince words. She called it like it was and there was no changing her opinion of things once she set her mind. "Look at me Linda," she hollered. My mother sat hunched over in her chair. She had been staring at the ground, but my aunt's tone startled her to lift her head.

"I'm sorry Bev. I'll do better next time." My mother stood and walked into the hallway.

"And you're still wearing your *goddamn* pajamas. I don't know how many times I need to tell you to get dressed in the morning. You make your bed, you eat your breakfast and take your pills." Aunt Bev walked over to my mother and grabbed her by the shoulders. "You have to fight this depression, Linda. You can't give in like this. I know losing Will was difficult but it's almost been a year now. You need to get it together."

It was hard to watch anyone be unkind to my mother, but I wanted her to snap out of it too. I wanted her to get better, to be better.

My mother blinked hard and tears fell fluidly down her cheeks. She struggled to get loose of my aunt's hold then walked into the bathroom, shutting the door firmly behind her. She rested her forehead on the wall and yanked a towel from the hook. I could see her chest move violently up and down she breathed, counting the moments for the anxiety to pass.

She stood in front of the sink. Her soft, slightly wrinkled skin had turned dull and shriveled from lack of sunshine and proper diet. Her hair needed cutting and her gray roots had been ignored for months. She stared at her image in the mirror and her face crumbled. My mother had always been very pretty, even with the mental problems that sometimes left her mind and body in disarray. She always looked decent and cared for herself in that way. But today, she looked like she felt: lifeless and lost.

She raised a shaking hand and reached to open the medicine cabinet. Inside was a small bottle of pills. She left her gaze on the bottle, staring hard, as if in deep reflection on the bottle's contents.

I knew what they were. Sleeping pills. She took them every night, mostly mixing them with wine before going to bed. Her nightly cocktail was the perfect mind-numbing alternative to her great pain.

She was considering an overdose and I needed to stop her, help her.

I flickered the lights on and off. She looked up at the ceiling and the light fixture but then seemed to lose interest. I filled the room with the bright light that streamed in from the small bathroom window. The quiet rays of sunshine beamed and bounced off the mirror, falling directly onto her face. I made sure that the sunrays were bright and that she could feel the warmth.

"You're stronger than you think, Mom. It's right around the corner, you have to hold on just a little bit longer. You've come this far. It'll get better, I promise you."

I watched her cry; staring at the bottle of medicine she slowly placed it back onto the shelf and shut the cabinet door.

"All right Mom! You did it. You did it. You put it back! You don't need it!" I moved all around, so proud of the strength she showed. I circled her body again like a twister, up and down my energy swirled. I wanted her to feel my pride. I wanted her to feel proud of herself. I looked into her face once more, and that's when I noticed the determination.

She smiled slightly and looked toward the door to the hallway. "Another time," she whispered and then she circled around to turn on the shower.

The room turned dark and I felt my energy drain. I felt my mother relax; the sleeping pills gave her peace of mind: She didn't have to suffer much longer if she decided not to.

It didn't work that way though, she didn't understand this.

She needed to banish the thought of suicide from her mind altogether.

I left my mother and searched for my aunt. Bev was sitting at the kitchen table, working on a crossword puzzle and writing out a to do list for my mother. I rounded the table fiercely.

"Why don't you help her?" I begged.

She looked up into the space between the table and the small chandelier that hung from the ceiling.

"Yeah, Bev! I'm talking to you! Why can't you help her?" I argued.

Bev looked confused but then lowered her head again to focus on her list. Her energy was negative and confrontational. She too had a darkened spirit, just like my mother.

I was frustrated, exhausted. I could feel I was starting to lose my energy and I had to get back to Heaven. I needed to retain what I had reserved and it was time for me to leave. I would have to explain this to my soul brother, but I did all that I thought I could do.

Time could only heal these wounds, and I was hoping that my mother had more time.

Lots and lots of time.

Chapter
Thirty-Two

The friendly waitress served eggs, toast, and hash browns, then refilled Alex and Rachel's coffee mugs. I could tell Alex was disappointed in how the previous evening had digressed, but I hoped that he wouldn't let that ruin their entire weekend.

They had gone to the Red Sox game and it looked like they were having fun. He took Rachel to dinner and they held hands as they walked down the sidewalk of Yawkey Way. The streets were crowded with fans and vendors; the energy in the atmosphere was musical. They purchased two dark blue Red Sox hats and two vintage Red Sox T-shirts so they both could match. Like twins, they interacted with ease and grace as they laughed effortlessly, enjoying each other's company.

"I missed you so much," he told her. She talked animatedly about her classes and the people she had met. Her eyes lit up when she smiled and the stress and sadness of my death that had originally bonded them in the first place seemed replaced by this love energy. Rachel was lovely, every little move she made.

They walked into the stadium and found their seats. Rachel grabbed his arm and pulled enthusiastically, "Should we get a drink?" she asked.

The line at the beer both was long and congested but Alex didn't disappoint her. "It may take a few minutes but, yeah, I'll get some drinks. What do you want?" he asked.

"A beer is good. A nice cold beer."

"Okay, I'll be right back. Hold our seats."

Before I died, Alex and I talked about getting fake IDs. Alex reached inside his wallet to retrieve his ID and I looked it over; the image of him was a good likening. We had spent hours together conspiring over our grand plan to be "twenty-one," and of drinking age.

"Can I have four beers please?" Alex handed over his license. The teller scanned it, then gave it back without question.

"That will be sixty dollars, please."

Alex choked on his gum, coughing. "Holy shit." He cringed as he paid for his drinks.

"Welcome to Fenway Park," the college-age man behind him replied.

Alex carried the drink tray back through the crowd and down to his seats where Rachel sat waiting. He handed her one of the four tall beverages and she raised an eyebrow at him. "Are you trying to get me drunk?" she teased.

"Oh my god, NO!" Alex laughed. "It's just that the line is so long."

"I know, I realize that. I'm really sorry, I could have gone without a beer, but it seems like it's the thing to do at ballgames."

"It's definitely the thing to do." Alex smiled. "Cheers!" He raised his cup and tapped it against Rachel's.

The crowd roared as the Red Sox played an incredible game against the Minnesota Twins. The first batter hit a homerun while bases were loaded, and the stadium rumbled with excitement. The music played loudly and the patrons stomped their feet as a wave started to move through the crowd. Rachel finished her first beer easily and began to drink her second one.

It was obvious to me that she started to feel tipsy. Her words slurred slightly and she slumped down in her seat at times, tired in this adorable way.

The game ended and Alex took Rachel's hand, leading her through the crowd, down several flights of stairs and back onto Yawkey Way. She was quiet for a while as they speed-walked up the street toward Alex's hotel, away from the packed sidewalks.

Alex turned back to look at her. Rachel attempted to smile at him, but she kept her head down mostly, and occasionally she took a deep breath of fresh air.

"Are you okay?" he asked. "I wanted to get out of there quickly. We would have gotten stuck in that crowd and I couldn't breathe."

Rachel looked at him with concern. "Oh no, I understand. I appreciate that. I just don't feel very good, that's all. I think I drank too much."

Alex placed his arm around her shoulders. "That was a lot of beer."

"I know." Rachel shrank. "I didn't want to waste it because it was so much money."

"How considerate of you," Alex teased. "What do you want to do now? My hotel is only a block away. We can go there, if you'd like?"

Rachel leaned into him and wrapped her arm around his waist for balance. "Would you mind taking me back to my dorm room?"

Alex's face fell. "Um, yeah, sure. Is everything okay?"

"I think it's probably better this way. I just don't feel good." Her face was getting pale and her breathing was accelerated. "I'm a really bad drinker," Rachel explained. "It never ends well; I'm such a lightweight," she joked.

"I feel awful about this. This is all my fault, really. Had I known you were such a lightweight, I would have brought you three beers instead of two. *Then* we'd be going back to my hotel room." Alex laughed at his joke. Rachel shoved him weakly, her balance and strength low.

They walked back to Rachel's dorm room and she slumped onto her bed. Alex helped her remove her shoes as she exhaled a sigh of relief.

She collapsed onto her pillow and he sat down next to her, moving her hair away from her face. Kissing her softly, he asked, "Can we meet tomorrow for breakfast?"

Rachel's eyes were already closed. "Um-hmm," she managed to say but she was falling asleep.

He kissed her again. "Good night, lightweight. I'll see you tomorrow," and then he reluctantly left the room.

Now he sat across from her in the diner and her eyes couldn't meet his.

"Last night was fun," Alex said.

Rachel rolled her eyes. "I'm so embarrassed."

"Don't be. It was fun. I had a great time actually."

Rachel looked at him with doubt. "What time are you leaving?" she asked as she took a bite of her pancake.

"I have to leave after breakfast."

"Oh," Rachel said, her face showing her disappointment.

"Maybe you can come home next weekend?" Alex asked hopefully.

"I can't. I have this project I'm working on with my friend Andrew. Do you remember Andrew Barlo? He went to school with us until the tenth grade and then his parents moved him to North Carolina."

"Yeah. Didn't you guys used to date?"

"Kind of, but that was a long time ago. He goes to school here and we were chosen to work together on this project. The assignment is eighty percent of our grade in my science class and we have this big presentation to do. We've been working on it all semester."

Alex twiddled with his fork. "You mentioned Andrew last night. He's a law student?"

267

"Yes, he's studying accounting and economics now but eventually he wants to go to law school. He's very determined and dedicated to his future and he's very smart. I feel a bit of pressure working with him." Rachel averted her eyes, her shoulders tense.

"Yeah, I can imagine."

"Anyway, I have to meet with him later."

The waitress came by and dropped the bill on the table. Alex placed twenty dollars back into the black check folder. He took Rachel's hand and walked with her out onto the sidewalk in front of the diner. The entrance to the T was a few steps away.

"Well, I guess this is goodbye then," he said as he handed her an envelope. "There's a little money inside. I know you need it. Please take it and buy a few pizzas for you and your friends."

Rachel lowered her eyes and her voice caught in her throat. "Why are you so good to me?" she managed as she reached out to hug him.

"I care about you," he whispered softly in her neck. All the positive encouragement his mother had given him just a few days earlier seemed to escape him, along with the words he wanted to say. She had inspired him to tell Rachel how he felt, but he said nothing. He held her back away from him. "If you need anything, please call me. I can help you, okay?"

Rachel's face fell. She kissed him one last time on his lips. "Thank you Alex," she said then turned and started to walk toward the entrance to the T station.

Alex stood there and watched her go. She wiped at her face with her arm.

Andrew Barlo. His energy was always pretty negative, if I remembered correctly. Alex was trying not to worry about it, but it was hard. He couldn't see her like he wanted to; he couldn't travel to Boston that often. It was too expensive.

Insignificant thoughts began to fill his head, and I watched him struggle to push those feelings and emotions aside. He was jealous and suddenly insecure, but of what he didn't understand.

There had been moments in Alex's life that he was not proud of: the times he had dismissed girls' feelings, or the times he had dated a girl and never returned her phone call, or the one night stands and the chasing he had done... It was all in him still, stuck in the back of his mind. What if karma was coming back to haunt him? What if it was his turn to feel hurt, to feel rejection or tossed aside?

I hoped that he would trust her and trust the energy that was between them.

He needed to push those negative thoughts aside and stay positive.

Chapter
Thirty-Three

Carol banged on my mother's front door for five minutes before she decided to go around the driveway and check the back door. She glanced at her watch and stood with her hands on her hips, impatiently waiting.

My mother lay in her bed, aware of the banging but ignoring it. Silently she asked Carol to go away, and then tried to move her lips to say the words. She kept trying but she hadn't spoken to anyone for several days and her throat felt stiff and dry.

"Go away," she whispered.

"Mrs. D? You in there? Mrs. D? I know you can hear me."

"Go away," she managed better this time.

The chimes on the door rattled as the banging continued. "I'm going to call the police if you don't come and open this door!" Carol leaned over the porch railing and tried to peek through the window. The blinds were shut tight and the glass had a film of pollen all over it.

My mother moved her legs, wincing with the pain, to swing them over the edge of the bed. Her eyes were closed, her brow furrowed in discomfort as she fumbled to put on her bathrobe. The alarm clock on her nightstand showed that it was 3:00 in the afternoon. Her back was hunched over as she pushed herself up off the bed and moved her feet across the grayish carpet. The hallway was dark but she didn't bother to turn any light on.

She stopped at the back door and lifted several blinds to peek through the window at Carol. "What?" she yelled.

Carol put her hand over her forehead and squinted to see. "Mrs. D? Please open the door. I'll only be a minute."

"I'm fine, Carol. I don't need any help right now, please go away." My mother turned and started to walk back down the hall toward her bedroom.

"It's important, Mrs. D. I received a letter for Will. It was delivered to me, and I didn't realize it until after I opened it. Actually, I think you should look at it," she stated, her voice muffled.

My mother stopped and was stilled by the mention of my name. She put a hand to her chest and cringed, as if someone had just stabbed her with a knife. She turned back and cracked the door, allowing Carol to slip the letter through the small opening. My mother closed the door abruptly in Carol's face.

"You're welcome!" Carol yelled as she stomped down the stairs. "Such a bitch," she muttered under her breath.

My mother gingerly bent over and clasped the letter against her chest. In my bedroom, she closed the door and sat on my bed. Lola had been sleeping but stood on my comforter to stretch her legs. She had turned into a beautiful dog; her coat was shiny and white with a random patch of black along her paws and her eyes. She was the only bright light in my mother's life, giving her energy of which my mother wasn't aware.

My room looked exactly the same. The closet still contained my clothing and my childhood trophies still lined my dressers. It had been over a year since I died, and nothing had changed in the room other than Lola making it her sleeping quarters. My mother held the letter up and tried to look through the envelope, as though the darkened room was going to shed some light on the information contained on the inside.

"Just open it," I said.

My mother started to cry. It was too much for her, my death. As much time as I spent with her and as much energy I was able to surround her with, none of it seemed to matter. She decided long ago that her life wasn't worth living—not without me anyway.

She cried. She put the letter on the bed and moved around the room, picking up my clothes and smelling them. Looking at the pictures hung on my wall of friends from the year before my death. My high school graduation picture was framed and sat proudly on my nightstand. She picked it up and kissed the glass.

She sobbed, holding tightly to the frame. I could see her body shake—all that sorrow and mournful energy still flooding her, creating a wave of anguish. She collapsed back onto my bed with a heavy thud, the letter just inches away from her hand.

"Open it," I said again. I realized she couldn't hear me or see me, but she could feel me, if she paid enough attention.

Finally, she quieted her sobs and reached for the letter. Her eyes were swollen and red. She pulled her reading glasses, on a chain around her neck, up to her eyes to read.

Dear Mrs. Daring,

We are pleased to announce that the Warriors for the Children Foundation have set up a scholarship fund in the name of your son, William A. Daring.

Donations in excess of over $10,000 have already been pledged! These funds will help sponsor many educational programs for the middle school and high school students, along with a yearly college scholarship for any deserving individual who successfully completes our "Stay Clean" campaign throughout their senior year.

We wish to invite you to a formal dinner on November 1ˢᵗ at the Litchfield County Inn, in which we will honor this year's scholarship recipient as well as promote the "Stay Clean" campaign, in the name of your son.

On behalf of our committee, please accept our deepest condolences to you. We hope that the programs we introduce will make a difference, bringing the young children of our community together in support and commitment to living more positive, healthy, and productive lives.

If you wish to contact me, please do so. I look forward to meeting you in person, and again, thank you very much for your time.

Sincerely,
Rebecca Hurly

Wow! This was really special. I watched her finish reading and then she quietly placed the letter back into the envelope. She walked back into her bedroom. She removed her bathrobe and threw it on the chair beside her bed.

"Mom! Do you realize how many kids this could help? How many students could get financial aid and continue on with their schooling? Do you realize how many lives could be saved if they could educate the younger students about the dangers of inhaling gasses and doing drugs? THIS IS INCREDIBLE!"

My energy glowed; I was optimistic that this type of positivity could make a difference for a young person, as well as for my mother. This was her chance to get involved, to be a part of the campaign. This was her chance to make a difference, to evolve above her mourning and to start showing love energy for her community. This was her chance to open a box, and who knows where this could lead her! My death didn't have to be in vain.

My mother climbed into her bed. She looked on the nightstand and reached for the pills my aunt had left for her. She took her sleeping aid and pulled the covers up high along her neck. She closed her eyes. She never smiled, not even once, at the news concerning the scholarship.

But I did. I was incredibly grateful.

Chapter
Thirty-Four

I followed Rachel as she rushed through campus and entered her dormitory, taking the stairs two steps at a time to the fourth floor. She was winded and out of breath but she made it to her room and threw herself on the bed.

I knew what she was feeling—I'd been there before. She was thinking that she wasn't good enough for Alex. Holding fear that if she hoped too much, she would be disappointed, torn between wanting and running. The attention he gave her made her feel safe and loved, but it also made her feel vulnerable, an uncomfortable feeling for her. I got it. She was holding on to the pain she felt from her stepfather. Maybe she couldn't understand why Alex liked her so much. Maybe she considered that perhaps he felt sorry for her. She and I, we never got a chance to say goodbye. But she and Alex...they were perfect for each other. I was so proud of Alex, the way he cared for her, and I hoped that she would remain open to the relationship, that she wouldn't close the box because of fear. They had genuine love between them, which was rare.

Rachel sighed. She sat up in her bed and placed her feet back on the ground. Grabbing her backpack off the desk, she slung it onto her shoulder, then walked back into the hallway of the student house. Several girls were crowded around a computer in the lounge area, looking through someone's social media, the squeal of high pitch voices bouncing off the cream-colored walls. Rachel smirked as she reentered the stairwell and made her way back down to the ground floor.

"I'm late," she mumbled to herself. She glanced at her watched and looked worried. "He's going to be so mad." She was on her way to meet Andrew.

Andrew suffered from his own unopened boxes but I couldn't explain this to Rachel; she had to figure him out on her own. His energy was negative and his ego was massive. He thought he was better than her, *definitely* smarter than her, but I could see who he was deep down: insecure and controlling. He was much like Rachel's stepfather Ray, so this was going to be a challenge for her. She would need to stand up for herself, not allow his energy to penetrate hers. She would have to navigate the situation by opening her own box.

The library was quiet as Rachel walked her usual path to the two small tables, located behind the sixth stack on the third floor. She passed the first few stacks and slowed down. Occasional sounds filtered through the space: a slow turning ceiling fan and the faint whisper of a library tech helping along a lost college student.

"I hope the tables are empty," she whispered to herself as she came around the corner. Her bag was full of her research notes and an organized marketing plan.

Andrew was there waiting, a look of irritation across his face. He glanced up at her briefly then continued to type on his laptop.

"Hello Andrew," Rachel said softly. "I'm sorry I'm late. I came as quickly as I could, but obviously not as quick as you." She laughed nervously.

His eyes remained busy and focused on his notes and he did not smile or reply.

"How was your weekend?" she asked cheerfully.

Andrew slammed his laptop shut and rubbed his temples and along the sides of his head. "I went to your dorm room last night."

Rachel looked up at him, surprised.

"You weren't there. I was hoping to see you and thought we could maybe get a jump start on the actual physical presentation portion of our assignment."

Rachel looked down, her cheeks flushed red. "I'm sorry, I was with a friend."

Andrew scrutinized Rachel's face. "Oh, what was her name?" he asked.

Rachel began to busy herself with her notes and took her own laptop out of her backpack and placed it on the table. She looked nervous, as if she were guilty of something, but she did nothing wrong to warrant his line of questioning.

"Don't let him make you feel this way," I whispered. She was trying badly to impress him, but whatever contributions she made to him or their project together never seemed good enough.

She stared at him oddly. "*His* name is Alex."

Andrew's stare was focused as his eyes began to dart back and forth from his laptop to her face. "Alex, huh?" he replied. Andrew stood from his chair and started to clear his side of the table.

Rachel watched in desperation. "Where are you going?" she asked fearfully.

Andrew paused before walking away. He turned and faced her. "My time is very valuable to me. I don't expect you to understand this, but I *have* to succeed in my life and this project is very important to me. Maybe you and I have different attitudes toward our schooling. I'm starting to regret the fact that I chose you to be my partner. At any rate, you lack the same motivation as I do and for right now, I'd like to work alone—on another floor even. Maybe tomorrow, if you get your act together, we can try to come together again on this project and maybe we could make it work."

Rachel's mouth fell open and she stood unblinking. She absorbed all his hurtful words and hard attitude toward her.

"He's jealous," I chimed in.

She cleared her throat and stood tall. "I'm very sorry that you feel that way toward me. I'm not sure exactly what I did to deserve such harsh words from you, but I was *only* ten minutes late. Perhaps maybe, Andrew, there is something *else* bothering you?"

Andrew thought for a moment. "I don't like you having a boyfriend. It's a distraction for you."

Rachel's head jolted back as she raised her hand and turned away from him. She didn't engage him. She sat back down in her chair and continued to look over the document pulled up on her computer. "I'm sorry you feel that way," she stated starkly. "Maybe tomorrow then?"

"Maybe," he stated then turned and walked out of their study area. Rachel took a deep breath.

She did the right thing, by not engaging him. They still had some time together though, and I could tell she was confused by his attitude toward her. Rachel was a beautiful person inside and out, but she had a hard time seeing it.

Andrew did not.

This was going to be a great lesson for her. A temporary relationship that teaches you important things about yourself, even though it was a negative experience for her, Andrew would help her grow.

Chapter
Thirty-Five

The scholarship dinner came and went and my mother refused to go. Aunt Bev was easily fooled by her explanations on how she didn't feel right celebrating my death. In fact, she called the foundation's good deeds "after the fact," as I had died and no one was there to help me. My mother didn't care about helping other people. She cared about herself and how her life had been impacted by my death. She couldn't see past her own scars.

Watching the interaction between them was like watching my favorite basketball team, in the last few minutes of a tumultuous rivaled game, start to lose their grip while the anticipation of a loss loomed and the clock ticked down to zero.

My aunt lingered cautiously, unsure if she trusted my mother. Her intuition was strong and accurate but she ignored those feelings and left my mother alone in the house to rest.

My mother's mind was calculated and focused, and every step she took from that moment further held purpose and determination. After my aunt left, my mother went into the kitchen, pulled out a bag of dog food, and filled every bowl in the house. She filled canisters with water and left treats scattered along the living room floor.

Lola came to her, her eyes aware and saddened by my mother's peculiar behavior. After a few minutes of affection, my mother said goodbye and then walked into the bathroom. She filled the bathtub with warm, deep water.

I knew what was happening, yet there was nothing I could do to stop it. I prayed for her. I prayed and prayed.

My mother stared at herself in the mirror. She touched her face and stretched her skin, distorting her appearance to make herself look as ugly on the outside as she felt on the inside. She inspected her graying hair and the wrinkles along her eyes and lips. Her chin quivered as silent tears fell down her cheeks. It was familiar to her, to feel such agony.

"Dear God help me," she whispered.

She was done feeling afraid and full of angst. The anxiety and depression never left her. She was done with missing me.

With quick movements, she stepped backward and lowered herself fully clothed into the warm bath water. She leaned back briefly and immersed herself, so that she was drenched from head to toe. Her face rose slowly from the porcelain tub, water dripping down her cheeks, a calm and serene grin on her lips.

"This is a very bad decision, Mom!" I screamed. I went to the edge of the tub and breathed all the light I could into her. *"This isn't how it needs to be! You have courage and purpose, Mom. You can do this. You can try harder!"* The depths of my energy frequency plummeted to almost nothing. The shadows of darkness filled the room and the light was quickly dissipating.

She leaned over the tub and picked up the small, portable radio I used to listen to while I showered. She plugged it in to an extension cord she'd brought in.

"Mom! Please!"

She raised the radio up over her head and paused, her hands shaking fiercely, her fingertips and knuckles white from exertion. Music came through, but the words were harsh and full of static, causing more chaos to an already desperate situation.

286

I tried to remember all the love that was in my mother. The affection she held for me, the way she nurtured me when I was young. I bestowed every positive thought I could think unto her, in hopes that it would sink into her mind and then into her soul. She needed to open herself to the bright light, even if it was a sliver of hope—even if it was just briefly. That one thing would bring her through the moment, so she could fight again the next day and the next day after, until the fight became the habit and the positivity became the norm.

She closed her eyes, then dropped the radio into the tub.

"No, Mom! Please!"

Sparks and flames shot out of the radio's speakers. My mother's body jolted into the space between the living and the dead and her soul fled her form, leaving her human remains to lie within the depths of the water.

The power blinked out.

I watched her cross over, her soul hovering over her own dead body as mine once did. The bathroom appeared as if it had been eclipsed by the night. I watched as the dark shadows crept through the cracks of the walls and I saw the bathroom floor open up, exposing a dark tunnel of molten rock, heading down into the depths of the earth. The darkened entities swirled around my mother's soul like a vacuum, pulling her down away from my light and into the hole. In an instant she was gone; her orb had faded and vanished, right before me.

I was weak, defeated by the evil forces that had won over my mother's intentions, and when I was summoned away from the space, I had no fight in me. Crossing back into Heaven, I had questions. Where were they taking her, the dark shadows? What was to become of her? What could I do to help her?

The heaviness I experienced was all around me and I felt hopeless and broken, unaware of exactly what had just happened. My soul brother came to me and walked me through my circumstance.

"Your mother committed suicide for what she thought would be an escape from her pain and reality." He entered into my aura, and our energies connected briefly into one ball of light. My spirit immediately felt recovery from his spirit and I basked in his unconditional love and understandings. "Her real suffering is about to begin now, for suicide is a spiritual crime. Her decisions are going to have an impact on her, not only ending her earthly life, but affecting her soul life too, and for eternity."

I asked him if there was anything that could be done.

"We will send her bright light, but it will be a difficult and long road for your mother's soul. She chose to escape from the lessons The Source had intended for her. What she didn't understand was that without the darkness of pain and suffering, there can be no light of healing and evolving. All the energy she held in her fear and tortured thoughts have been locked inside her now, never to be healed and never to be freed, existing in an eternity of pain and misery. She didn't escape the agony by committing suicide, she created a jail for herself."

My soul brother loved me unconditionally, and he drew upon his own energy to lift mine toward an enlightened state of awareness. Together we sent my mother bright light, and supported by my soul family, they and others joined us in our quest to help save her. I could feel the resistance of the dark energy—the screaming and growling of an entity not willing to let her go, for her dark energy was like fuel to their fire. Our love grew stronger and stronger for her, but so did their hatred, anger, and desire.

Time seemed endless as my soul brother eventually stepped out of my aura, softening his light. My soul family gathered around us, waiting for him to communicate.

"They've got a hold on her so tight, because she is still so weak."

I could feel the dark energy and the strength it had as it pulled on her.

"We won't give up. We have an eternity to save her soul. It's going to take a long time and much patience, but we will help her heal, and she will get stronger."

I thanked my soul brother for the help he was willing to give and the love energy he held for my mother's soul.

Thoughts weighed heavily on me: what I had done to *myself* and now what my mother had done. The mistakes she made were permanent and could not easily be undone. It dawned on me how fortunate I was that I was given a second chance to heal and evolve.

Love energy had saved me. Hopefully, love energy would save my mother.

Chapter
Thirty-Six

Rachel lost her focus staring at the wall; the information she received from Alex was devastating. My mother, Linda, had died.

Sadness filtered through my family again, as my aunt was left to cope with another disturbing tragedy. Aunt Bev suffered through so many things in her lifetime, yet she still continued on. I didn't appreciate her enough while I was alive, but man, she held an undying strength in her spirit.

Alex went on about how he should have visited my mother more often and how he had let me down. Rachel tried her hardest to comfort him. He was close to my mom, and he felt responsible in many ways that he was unable to help her.

"I can't come home Alex. I wish I could, but I can't." Rachel closed her eyes as the guilt settled across her face. Alex needed her, but her project presentation was due and classes were winding down for the week. She couldn't disappoint Andrew.

"I understand," he said solemnly.

"I promise, next weekend I'll come for a visit. I'm really sorry I can't be there for you, Alex. I'll make it up to you, I swear."

There wasn't much she could do for him. Schoolwork was her priority. Andrew was content for once with the quality of her note cards and had actually praised her for the first time, the night before. He even brought her a coffee, which he never did. Maybe he was changing. Anything was possible.

She picked up the phone and dialed her mother.

"Hello?" The stern and unwavering voice of her stepfather rang through the phone line.

Rachel's shoulders slumped. "Hello sir," she answered.

"Hello Rachel. It's fairly late; shouldn't you be in class already?"

"Yes sir. Class starts at 8:30. I was hoping to catch Mom before she went to work. Is she there? Can I speak with her?"

"No, I'm sorry. She left already."

Rachel exhaled deeply. I could tell she missed her mother. It was rare that she caught her alone without her stepfather but when she did, they had open and loving conversations. When I was alive I couldn't quite figure out why her mother stayed with such a domineering man. Now I knew she was never able to heal from the fact that Rachel's real father had left them.

"Oh, okay then."

"Well, what is it? I can relay the message to her."

Rachel hesitated. This wasn't a conversation for him, but he would get angry with her if she didn't answer his question.

"My friend William's mother died. I wanted Mom to know."

"William? The friend that died last year?"

"Yes sir."

"That's unfortunate."

"Yes, it is. Anyway, I'll call back tonight. Can you tell Mom that I called for her?"

"How did she die, Rachel?" he asked.

Silence lingered over the phone line. "The authorities suspect that she may have killed herself in her bathroom, but this hasn't been confirmed to me by anyone from the family. I'm not sure of the details, exactly."

Her stepfather breathed heavily with irritation. "Are you surprised?" he asked. "These were weak people." Ray didn't know my family or didn't even care to know my family.

"Anyway, I have to go now," Rachel said. "I'll be late for class."

"Wait one minute," he stated firmly. "Answer my question. Are you surprised?"

"Yes sir, I am. I am very surprised and sad that this happened to his family. I feel terrible for them."

Ray's condescending laughter made my stomach turn and I felt badly for Rachel. Her face was red with anger and I could see her chest heave as she buried her feelings inside, unwilling to confront him.

"Can I go now?" she asked.

"You kids have no idea what the real world is like. Something so tragic, and you feel sad and devastated. Bad things happen all the time, Rachel. I think it's time you start getting used to it. You can't run to your mother and me every time something awful happens. You need to start dealing with these things on your own."

Rachel's mouth dropped open. I could feel years of frustration building in her throat, her voice begging her to react. She took a deep breath.

"I will call and contact my mother anytime that I wish to," she said. "I didn't call to have a conversation with you or to ask you for your support. In fact, you were the last person I wanted to talk to. I prayed that you wouldn't answer the phone!"

The silence was thick and Rachel tried desperately to hold her tears. He was hurtful, always so hurtful and uncaring.

"You've never been grateful," he stated coldly.

"And you've never been loving. Do you know what I feel is truly sad and tragic? *You.* I think you are tragic. You have no friends, no family that comes to you. My mother is the only thing that you have, and someday she too may leave you to your miserable self. I've spent years trying to make you happy, and you've disappointed me, time and time again. I don't want to have these conversations with you anymore. I don't want *anything* to do with you."

Rachel covered her mouth with her shaking hands, her eyes squeezed tightly. I couldn't believe the words that slipped out of her mouth. I was so proud of her. *Don't say you're sorry; don't take your words back. Express how you truly feel.* It was time she stopped taking his abuse; it was time she spoke her words.

"The feeling is mutual, Rachel. I would have had children of my own, if it weren't for you. But instead, I gave all my time and energy to raising you, and you're nothing but a spoiled little girl with hurt feelings."

Rachel gasped. "I'm sorry that I've been a huge disappointment to you, but you've been an even bigger one to me."

"Goodbye, Rachel." Her stepfather hung up.

Rachel shook her head and reluctantly turned the phone off.

She walked to class, a clouded expression on her face. I wondered how her mother was going to react when they spoke. Her stepfather was controlling and manipulative, so it was possible that Rachel might have made her mother's life more difficult. She had never really expressed to her mother how she felt about her stepfather.

Maybe now was the time. Maybe things would change. Maybe *she* would matter.

Chapter
Thirty-Seven

I didn't have to wonder long. When Rachel walked out of class and checked her cell phone, she had five missed calls from her mother.

Her eye twitched, her expression of dread apparent. She held on to her stomach, looking nauseous. The stress was all over her.

I thought about the morning she had—how Alex had called with the horrible news about my mom and then the unexpected confrontation with her stepdad. Maybe she could put her mother off, just until after she met with Andrew. The presentation was scheduled for 2:00 that afternoon. Rachel looked at her watch. It was 11:30, which gave her just enough time to meet with Andrew to review, eat a small lunch, then head to her classroom. She ignored her mother's phone calls. She might regret that decision later, I knew, but she was too focused on the presentation. Her energy was motivated to succeed.

She stopped at her dorm room and changed into attire that was more appropriate for her speech: a black skirt and white button-down shirt. She slipped on a pair of heels and neatly tied her hair away from her face. Her makeup was subtle with an added shade of soft pink lip gloss. She looked beautiful.

Her presentation was neatly packed away into the small briefcase that carried her laptop. *"You're going to be late, Rachel,"* I said. Her watch revealed the impending time ticking.

She hurried, as fast as one could hurry in a pair of high-heeled shoes. As she made her way through campus, Rachel cursed herself for not wearing a pair of flats. She entered the school library just as the 12:00 church tower bells began to ring.

Andrew was there of course, in a nicely pressed white shirt with black tie. He smiled at her, pleasantly. They sat together and went over the minor details of the presentation. Andrew was nervous; I could tell by the way he tapped his pencil on the wooden desk table. Rachel's face surprisingly revealed a calm smile, and I imagined that she felt relief that this project was coming to an end which would leave her more time to deal with her mother and to be there for Alex.

She stood next to Andrew and rehearsed her portion of the presentation. Science was an easy subject for her and astronomy was one that had intrigued and captivated her attention ever since she was a little girl.

When we were young, sitting next to each other in science class, we worked on our shoebox project for weeks. She beamed with pride as she walked the completed project up to the front of the class: The array of hanging planets surrounded the sun, blackened by the night of sky, tucked away in a large shoebox. Her projects quality far exceeded that of our classmates. Science was her specialty.

The extra time she spent trying to please Andrew, writing and rewriting her note cards and material, practicing and focusing on the level of perfection that he expected from her, left her prepared and she performed the practice presentation flawlessly. Her language flowed naturally, she did not stumble on her words, and she was even able to ad-lib a little humor in her explanations.

Andrew was not prepared.

When he stood alongside Rachel, imagining that they were presenting in front of the teacher and the class, the fear was evident on his face. The lack of concentration settled into his uneasy eyes as he stared at his notecards. Rachel stepped back and let him continue, also witnessing his body language and his lack of confidence. Andrew was clearly irritated, shuffling his note cards. He narrowed his eyes as he spoke condescendingly, interrupting his own part of the presentation to criticize Rachel for the way she stood while she read her notes, and the way she moved around while she spoke. He imitated her speech in an inaccurate and over-exaggerated tone. He pointed his finger at her. *"You're* going to screw this up."

Rachel's face flushed red all over. The presentation wasn't complete yet but she looked more anxious over her partner than the presentation itself. He was jealous. I could feel it. I hoped she recognized it too. It explained everything—how he was so verbally negative toward her; he was jealous of her.

"Andrew, please. This is hard enough without the negativity. You're doing great. Why don't you sit for a minute and clear your mind. I think you've worked yourself up to the point where you can't concentrate on what's important. If you continue to think negative thoughts, you're going to have a negative result. You need to stay positive."

Andrew sat in a chair and continued to open and close his books, slamming papers down, mumbling under his breath. "This has been a failure, right from the get-go. We should have never been partners."

"It's too late for that now Andrew. We need to get ready and go to class. Maybe the walk and fresh air will do you good."

Rachel started to gather her material, watching him. He wiped his forehead with a cafeteria napkin. His shirt was damp around his armpits. He stood and put on his sport jacket. He took his notes and packed his things. They walked toward their lecture hall in silence.

I thought about Alex. He was always so strong and confident. He knew what he wanted; he worked hard and he wasn't afraid of things. Alex showed respect to people. A much different sentiment than what I was feeling from Andrew.

Rachel glanced at Andrew. His face was stern and angry, his anxiety and negativity ruining him. Her grace and preparedness was going to have to carry them through their presentation. She stood tall and confident. She took several steps in front of him and walked ahead, leaving him behind to fester.

The classroom was crowded with other students who had their presentations out and ready. Rachel and Andrew were second on the list of presenters.

They stood together, in front of the class. Andrew spoke first briefly, and then looked at Rachel, terrified.

She smiled at him. "Thank you Andrew, for the perfect introduction." She knew her material—and she knew Andrew's, too.

Andrew stared confused but then carefully stepped aside, allowing Rachel to continue.

Presenting on both of their behalf, Rachel spoke fluent astrology, her words leaving her tongue flawlessly, and as she drew their presentation to a close, the classroom erupted in a round of applause. The energy in the room was invigorating. I felt so much pride for her; she was strong and confident. She smiled as though her cheeks would crack. The teacher thanked her and expressed to her what a great job she had done.

She bowed slightly then returned to her seat, radiant.

She nailed it.

Chapter
Thirty-Eight

Andrew and Rachel parted ways after class. He thanked her, but his gratitude lacked sincerity and his energy remained negative. I felt empathy for him, but couldn't help him find his way. I imagined that there was a lot of pain in him, things I couldn't understand and hoped that he would heal himself in some way, eventually opening himself up to a higher vibration of love and positivity. He needed to believe in himself. He needed to open some boxes.

Rachel dialed Alex's number and he answered on the second ring.

"Hey," she said softly. She ducked behind one of the campus buildings and found a lone bench she could sit on. She took off her shoes and stuck her feet on the warm concrete, letting the sun bathe her in warmth and light.

"Hi!" his voice came through on the phone. "This is a nice surprise! Is everything okay?"

I remembered how many times Alex had listened to her talk about me and the mysteries of life, how much shame she felt about her relationship with her mother and stepfather.

"I finished the presentation."

"Oh yeah? How did it go? You must be relieved."

"It went well actually, very well. I think I did a good job," she said, grinning. "I left the classroom afterward, and all I could think about was hearing your voice." She paused. "Today feels like a hard day, in other ways, and I'm sorry that I'm calling, but I needed to hear you, and so, anyway..."

Alex remained quiet on the other end. Finally, he spoke. "Come home, Rachel. I can meet you at the train station. Even if for only one day, we can sit together and talk. I know you have a lot on your plate, but I'd like to see you."

I saw her eyes well up with tears, which then rolled down her cheeks—the emotions she had been suppressing all day. Her pain was evident in the way her lips trembled and her voice cracked, but with Alex, it didn't matter. She could cry if she wanted to. He would only love her more. "It's my mom and stepdad... I created a situation that needs handling. I'm not sure what I'm going to do. I wish someone could tell me how to manage this, because I feel a little lost."

"Your stepfather is such an asshole."

Rachel started to laugh. We all knew that this was true, but it was funny to hear Alex react on her behalf.

"I mean, I don't get it. You are like the most perfect person that I know. You are sincere and genuine in every way possible, and still, he treats you like garbage."

Rachel smiled. "Well, I appreciate those lovely compliments. I think that I received a good lesson today, in jealousy. Andrew's been really rotten toward me and for some reason it clicked today. I think he's been jealous of me. His behavior is so similar to my stepdad's. They're both so negative and I feel like I've been an easy target all these years, but I'm not."

"Andrew? That dirtbag? What did he do to you? Because I'll have a delicate conversation with him, if you want me to."

"No, please…it's over now. I don't have to deal with him anymore. He wasn't very good during the presentation and I think that was punishment enough for him. It doesn't matter now. I'm just making the observation and sharing it with you."

"Your stepfather doesn't understand you. You should be proud of yourself, even if he isn't. I can see what you do and who you are, and I'm very proud of you too."

I watched Rachel's light within her brighten, her heart overflowing with warmth. "Thank you, Alex. I really appreciate that. I feel much better having talked with you. I'll think about coming home within the next few days. I have to call my mother. It's not going to be easy."

"Okay, let me know when you're coming. I'll be there waiting for you. I can't wait to see you, Rachel."

"Me too, Alex."

"Hey Rach?"

"Yeah?"

"I love you, sweetheart."

Rachel leaned back on the bench, a slight smile surfacing as she played with her hair, wrapping it around her fingers.

"I love you too, Alex. I'll see you soon."

"Okay. See you soon."

Rachel hung up the phone.

She started to walk back to her dorm room. Moving past the cafeteria, she came upon a small crowd gathered around a temporary stage and speaking podium.

"What's going on?" she asked.

"This is incredible," a classmate said. "Professor Crawford is giving a speech today on her new book, *Finding Your Voice*. Have you heard of it, have you read it?"

I was pleased to watch Rachel sit down and listen. "I haven't heard of the book, but this sounds very interesting," she said.

The speaker cleared her throat. "How many people here have heard of the word 'vibes'? Show me your hands," the professor asked.

Hands flew up in the air.

"That's right. We use the word 'vibes' all the time. You may say, 'Hey, that girl has great vibes' or 'Man, I didn't like his vibes at all.'" The professor placed her hands sharply on her hips and wrinkled her nose. "Does anyone here know what the word actually means?"

The crowd remained silent.

"Vibes is short for vibrations, and the rate at which vibration occurs is also known as a *frequency*. We are all energy, vibrating frequencies." Professor Crawford paused. "This is not an unknown phenomenon to most of you students, especially the science buffs. We all

307

vibrate and we all have frequencies, including your thoughts and emotions."

I nodded in agreement with her.

"Does anyone here experience anxiety?"

Again, a small amount of hands went up in the air. Rachel raised her hand as well.

"As students, I'm sure some of you experience similar emotions such as fear, worry, and doubt. You may be worried about a test you're about to take or you may doubt you'll pass a certain class...or other stressful, temporary feelings. These are what I call 'low vibe' energies. These low-vibe emotions and thoughts can manifest in many ways, but in my experience, anxiety has been the most common manifestation. It affects almost every person you know. Other emotions such as jealousy, guilt, insecurity, anger, frustration, and depression are also known as 'low vibing' energies."

Rachel sat up in her chair when she heard the word *jealousy.*

The professor pointed at the crowd. *"Anxiety* is your body's way of telling you that your frequency is too low. It is your body's way of rejecting those vibes, helping bring awareness to your thoughts, and encouraging you to change your thinking from negative to positive. The goal is to vibrate as high a frequency as possible. Positive vibes such as love, courage, hope, optimism, peace, and joy raise the body's vibration and can manifest in a way that can lead your spirit to your best possible life."

Students all around were nodding their heads.

"How do we change our thoughts then?" Professor Crawford looked around at all the students' faces. "It's quite simple, really. It's like anything else—you have to practice and train and have an awareness. Instead of *worrying* that you will fail an exam, train your mind to believe that you will pass the exam with flying colors. Of course, you *do* need to study." The crowd laughed, and she continued: "Instead of *dreading* going to an 8:00 AM Saturday class, wake up with enthusiasm and walk into the classroom with energy that inspires people."

One student yelled out, "That's impossible!"

Professor Crawford laughed. "You see? Negative vibes! *Everything* is possible, my friend. You just have to set your mind to it." The professor paused. "Negative thoughts can lower your vibration and frequency, and can cause anxiety. Have you ever met someone who never gave love? Whose miserable and negative attitude can be felt all the way across the room and you just wanted to get away from that person?"

Under her breath Rachel muttered, "Is this woman in my head?" Everything Professor Crawford spoke about were things that were pertinent to her and her current situation. "This must be a coincidence."

I thought this woman was brilliant. How could Rachel change the predicament she was in? She was never going to change her stepfather, but she could change her own reaction to the situation. She could change her thoughts.

"People who are not on the same vibrational frequency will distance themselves from you, while those who are on the same frequency will come toward you. It's called the law of attraction. Positive vibes attract positive vibes. Negativity attracts negativity."

Rachel seemed to be getting the answers to her problems, just ten minutes after she asked. Light bulbs were going off all around the crowd and a calm and serene energy washed over the classmates.

The crowd, including Rachel, was getting answers from the universe. She didn't need to feel alone. She was doing the right things...and I think for the first time in her life she understood that she and her stepfather were never going to "vibe."

She returned to her dorm room, ready to make that phone call.

Chapter

Thirty-Nine

Rachel sat on her bed and closed her eyes. She meditated, repeating delicately, "My stepfather needs understanding. I will remain positive even when he is negative. My vibes are hope and appreciation."

She picked up the phone and dialed her mother.

"Rachel?"

"Hey, Mom," Rachel spoke with calmness and confidence. I was optimistic that she was going to smooth things over for her mother's sake.

"Hey sweetheart, how are you?" Her mother was also calm, which surprised me. Perhaps Rachel had worried for no reason at all. "I was trying to get a hold of you. I heard about William's mother. Are you okay, honey? I know that must have been a shock for you."

Rachel's face scrunched up as she sucked in her bottom lip. The mention of my mother was a reminder of how complicated life could be. It was a difficult example of how low my mother's vibe was and how helpless it felt, that no one could save her.

"Oh yeah, it was, Mom. I feel so sad for his family. It's hard to believe and understand, but I'm okay. I'm dealing with it."

"Good, Rachel. There's not much you can do about it anyway. I worried about you all day. I hoped that this news about Will's mom wouldn't be devastating for you."

Maybe Ray didn't tell her about their previous conversation.

"Thanks, Mom. I was shocked when I heard the news and I felt the sadness, but I'm okay. Thank you for your concern." Rachel paused. "Is Ray there? Can I speak with him?" She waited for her mother to hand the receiver over to her stepfather.

"Hey," Rachel stated strongly a moment later. "I realize that I'm the last person you want to speak to right now, but I feel the need to apologize. I appreciate everything you've done for me over my lifetime. I value the hard work you do and the fact that you've provided me with a safe and secure upbringing. I am grateful for the sacrifices you've made to help raise me. You're a decent man, Ray. We may never be able to show our love and affection for one another, but I do respect you, and I hope that you can accept this apology from me and that we can move forward, in a positive way." Her bravery was inspiring. I realized that this was a difficult conversation for Rachel to have, but she was doing it, and I was so proud of her.

Rachel's stepfather tried to speak, his voice shaking slightly with emotion. "I do love you, Rachel. I wouldn't be so hard on you if I didn't love you and want to protect you. As a young female, you may not understand the rough and tough ways of an old, retired military man, but my intentions were never to hurt you, but to keep you strong and protected."

He was high vibing on her! He said he loved her!

Rachel closed her eyes, relief evident in the way her muscles relaxed in her face and her body dropped, no longer rigid, but content.

"Thank you Ray. I love you too." She wiped the tears from her eyes.

"And I am sorry about your friend's mother. It really is an awful thing, to lose a child. I couldn't imagine losing you and the pain she must have been suffering from."

Rachel exhaled, I was amazed and grateful for the level at which she and Ray were communicating. Maybe she had grown in the last day; maybe he considered her an adult now and would treat her as such. Whatever was happening was encouraging and I could see her boxes align with who she was and who she wanted to be, as a person. She was strong, she was amazing and lovely in so many wonderful ways.

"I really appreciate that, Ray. Thank you for listening and giving me the opportunity to apologize. I need to go now, but say goodbye to Mom for me, okay? I'll see you guys soon."

"Okay Rachel. Have a good night."

Rachel ended the call, then dialed Alex. He didn't answer but she left him a message.

"Hey, it's me. It's around 5:00. I'm coming home. I hope you get this message soon. I should be there at the train station, around 8:00. Please meet me!"

Rachel packed a small bag of her things. She walked to the train station and her spirit soared with a renewed sense of freedom. She was going home and for the first time in a long time, her smiled revealed that she was looking forward to it.

Chapter

Forty

Things were happening faster than I could keep up. It was time to say goodbye to my friends and family. Aunt Bev was shutting down my mother's house and placing it on the market to be sold. She was closing a sad chapter in her life with the loss of my mother and me, but Bev was strong and solid. She spoke of the foundation with her friends and as a schoolteacher, I knew Bev held a special place in her heart for students. She was starting to see where she could make a difference and her boxes were aligning. She would be a great asset to the foundation. I blessed her and thanked her; I was proud.

Carol spoke from her porch as Bev began to get into her car. "You're selling the house?" she asked.

"Yes, it's time to move on."

"I'm very sorry for your loss," Carol said. "It's so sad, what happened here."

"Yes it is. Thank you. What about you, Carol? What are you going to do now?"

"I'm going back to school. I've been clean for thirty days and my mother is moving in with me to help me with the kids. I'm trying to create a better life for my children and myself. I feel hope right now for the first time in a long time." Carol's smile was bright.

"I wish you the best, Carol. Good luck and stay in touch, if you need me."

"Thank you, Bev. You too."

The energy surrounding my mother's house seemed to change now that my mother was gone. I could feel a glimpse of hope for Carol and her children, which was important. I said goodbye and moved along.

I sat with Rachel on the train and watched her stare out the window. Her spirit was awakened now, and so was Alex's. The love energy was strong but so was her curiosity. She was beginning to feel the light within her flash with hope and an interest to discover how the universe really worked. Awakenings were beautiful journeys and I was excited for her and Alex, my two best friends. It was amazing to watch the beauty of love that the spirit guides and angels held for their human counterparts. It was unconditional, the gifts they would give, the dreams they could make true, and the guidance they offered. All the human spirit needed to do was to trust in the divine process. They needed to believe in something bigger than themselves.

Rachel's energy was calm and content and she felt strong, stronger than ever before. Positivity was flowing her way; her vibes were high and full of optimism for the future. She loved Alex and was willing to be vulnerable with him, to let him love her and to love him back just as strongly. She was grateful.

I told her that I loved her, that her soul was beautiful and that we were family, her and I. Soul family.

***

The train decelerated to a slow stop. Rachel reached for her bag on the side of the seat and a cool rush of air flowed up her arm. Sudden goose bumps appeared on her skin. She paused, intuitively registering that something had just happened, but she couldn't quite put her finger on it.

She stood and walked toward the doors, stepping out onto the platform, looking for Alex. The train emptied behind her as other passengers made their way toward the staircase, down to the main street and parking areas.

She walked toward the stairs and as she started to descend, Alex met her halfway up, out of breath, having taken the stairs two at a time. Looking down at his feet, he barely noticed her until he almost bumped into her.

"Alex!" Rachel exclaimed. The smile on his face said everything. It was as if she was seeing him again for the very first time and feeling his energy penetrate hers, in a new and amazing way.

They stood facing each other. He moved his hand along her cheek and placed it gently on the back of her neck. They remained speechless as the breath in their lungs synced with each other, their eyes penetrating each other's soul with intensity and love energy.

He leaned into her and kissed her mouth with the gentleness of a butterfly. Rachel wrapped her arms around his neck. They stood on the stairs, enveloped in each other.

A man's voice came over the train station intercom. *"Last call for Boston. Train 111 will be departing in five minutes."*

Alex released Rachel. "You're never going back." Rachel laughed but his message was clear: They were going to be together.

I swirled around them with the grandest of blessings that I could and said goodbye, my soul being called back once again, to Heaven.

It was time for ascension.

My soul family was waiting for me as I entered the space from which we all come. The light filled the room and energy swirled around like a tornado, cleansing me and clearing my spirit for a new and exciting adventure. My guardian angel was there, overseeing the soul contracts that were being formulated and signed. We discussed my next life adventure—who would be my parents, who were to be my spirit guides to help encourage me along my path. My best friends were chosen for me, along with my enemies too.

"What would be the greatest journey you could imagine, Will? What would you like to experience this time around?" my soul brother asked.

"Love energy." I had no doubt that I wanted to fall in love. "I want to be a father and I want children."

"Excellent, Will. Perhaps in this lifetime, you will meet another soul mate or your twin flame."

"What's a twin flame?" I asked.

My soul brother shuffled me along. "Enjoy the experiences, Will. Hold on to faith and lead with love, and always remember, love is where you come from."

It was time for me to be reborn, to learn my next level of lessons and to go on another earthly pilgrimage, to be human again.

I wanted this. I asked for it. I prayed for another chance…and since it was the mission of the spirit guides to make dreams come true, my soul family happily granted me this opportunity.

I was to be born again.

The End.

Suicide Help Lines

1-800-273-8255

Addiction and Mental Health Help Lines

1-800-662-4357